A COYBOY'S VOW

KATE CONDIE

To Michelle, Kimberly, Sadie, Taryn, Kelly & Courtney. My dedicated beta readers who gave their time, their opinions and helped me when I doubted myself.

1

I vete hurled a sigh at the train car window. The dense trees flew by, but it would be more than a day before they would arrive on her brother's ranch in the Montana Territory. Once there, her mother could focus her criticism on someone else for a change. Her mother's voice came from the upholstered bench beside her. "Don't be such a child. All men do it, and your Henry will learn to be more discreet. The key is to *act* outraged. He'll learn to keep it from you in the future."

Ivete ground her teeth. Maybe when her brother's baby was born, her mother would be so busy playing grandmother she wouldn't have time to lecture Ivete about how a marriage didn't need to include devotion.

At her mother's words, Ivete's mind filled with the woman who had approached her with tear-filled eyes. Claimed she was Henry's lover and spat on Ivete's dress.

Ivete studied her mother's profile, waiting for understanding to dawn, or possibly for her mother to say this was all some cruel joke. That Ivete wouldn't be expected to marry a man who doled out affection whenever it took his fancy. "He wasn't the one who told me, Mother. How could he know she would approach me?" Ivete remembered the hurt in the woman's eyes. Pain that spoke of a love for Henry that Ivete had never possessed. Ivete shook her head. Whatever that woman shared with Henry, it wasn't the transactional encounter Ivete's mother had described: money given for services Ivete blushed to think about.

The enamored woman's love was unrequited. When Ivete had confronted Henry, he promised to give her up. It was strange, but his surrender caused Ivete to despise the man. A shred of pity for that woman had wriggled its way into her core. The woman, no matter her profession, was too good for Henry. Too good for the men and women who fed such an industry, treating it as though it were one of the many new factories lining the streets and pockets of the Chicago elite, churning out products for consumers. Only this product could feel pain, both at its use and when the time came, its neglect.

Out the window, the vast expanses of browns and golds gave way to greener valleys and forests. The trees were unlike anything Ivete had ever seen. Not even the lands around her grandparents' home in the country were this lush. Bastien's letter telling the family he'd found a ranch for himself and his wife was the final blow for Ivete. He would never shake off his odd ideas. He'd rejected their family ways entirely, and his rejection left her like a boat at the regatta with no wind in her sails. She had hopes of him moving his wife back to Chicago, of setting up house near the Graham family home and once more being her closest brother. Instead, she and her mother were going to spend more than a month in the wilds of Montana helping care for Bastien's new babe.

Her mother's comments continued, like an insect

hitting the window as it attempted to fly free. Except instead of some mindless creature, Ivete was the one caged, stuck in this train while her mother pressed her advantage. "It is no secret Henry is a catch. When you marry money, you must learn to endure the jealousy of others."

Ivete faced mother. "This isn't about jealousy. He had a relationship with that woman, and she loved him. You didn't see her face." Ivete shook her head at her mother's refusal to see Ivete's side.

"Be glad I didn't. It's already all over town. You had enough witnesses to your disgrace."

Ivete's cheeks burned. "My... Mother, surely you don't mean that."

"Dealing with difficult people is a lady's job. I fear I haven't given you enough chances to practice. I should have given you charge of the household before ever allowing you to be courted."

Her mother's habit of bashing into the wrong wall was insensible, and Ivete's ears grew hot at the conversation. *My disgrace. As though I had driven Henry into another woman's arms.* Society expected she never be alone with him; yet somehow, it was within her power to have prevented the affair.

The train's metal wheels squealed against the track, launching both women forward to brace against the tabletop. After a few moments the train stopped entirely, and they settled into their seats again, their eyes wide as they looked at one another. The sound of the abrupt stop rang in Ivete's ears.

A rider, a bandana covering all but mean, squinting eyes, galloped along her side of the train. Her heart beat a rhythm in her chest. She longed to cross the cabin and see if they were on the other side. Was it possible for a moving train to be surrounded?

"Mother, look." Both women leaned into the window, trying to see if there were any more masked men.

Shouting came from beyond the doors to their private cabin. When the door burst open, both women jumped as a dusty man stepped inside. A scrap of fabric covered his nose and mouth and muffled his speech. He waved a pistol as he spoke, his finger along the side as though he didn't expect to use it in this cabin. "This is a robbery, ma'am. Give me everything of value, and we'll be on our way." The casual, low drone made it appear as if he were bored. Ivete cocked her head as she assessed the man. He was nothing like she'd imagined from the descriptions in her favorite novels. Her heart set to a gallop as she remembered the scenes she'd read of dashing robbers stealing girls from their wagon train.

Ivete's mother shot up, not to defend their belongings but to remove all jewelry from her body. She worked the clasp on her necklace and turned a sharp voice on her daughter. "Ivete. Now."

The fear that coursed through her veins served to focus her actions. Ivete stayed in her seat as she slid the earrings from her lobes, each of them making a faint click as metal connected at the closure. She'd worn them at her first ball and recalled the candlelit hall every time she put them on. Next was a simple string of pearls her father had given her on her sixteenth birthday. Had four years passed already? It didn't seem so long ago that she'd been hoping to be twenty, the age her parents promised she could marry and be given her inheritance. Now she was of age, and all her plans had withered. She would rather stay in Montana with its dusty robbers and drab colors than marry Henry.

As she thought of her fiancé, she slid the engagement ring from her finger. The ring snagged on her knuckle but slipped off easily once past that widest point. She shed the ornament as a fisherman removes a hook from the lip of his catch. Though the bandit waved his pistol at her to hurry, the release she felt as she dropped the band into his waiting palm was physical. When she returned her empty hands to her lap, she couldn't tell if she was the hook, dangling free on a line with nothing to weigh it down. Or perhaps she was the fish flopping on the shore and hoping its wild efforts would take it back to the safety of the water. She might be untethered, but not free. Never free. She scooped from her skirt the rest of her treasures, bits of jewelry that were a journal of her life. She passed them to the man and knew she could buy more. She could forget her past and start anew. Her fiancé had more than enough money to buy her anything she wanted, be it a pearl necklace or a gilt carriage. What he didn't possess was the ability to make her forget.

"Have a good day, missus." The bandit raked his gaze down Ivete's frame before tipping his hat and turning for the door.

Once he was gone, her mother let out a huff. "Your father won't let us travel again, not if the law can't get these robberies under control. That man looked in every way as though he was doing us a favor."

"Maybe he was." The bandits in the dime novels were much worse, drawing their guns at every opportunity, kidnapping the rich for a ransom or the young to be sold. Ivete couldn't deny the twinge of disappointment at having experienced something she'd read about so many times. Like many things in life, the reality didn't live up to the imagination. She thought of her dreams for a wedding and a husband. He would be prince charming. Rich, handsome, and doting. Henry *was* all those things— when he was with her. Did the fairy tales ignore the side story that Charming went to the club after a hard day fighting dragons. That he paid a woman for services Ivete blushed to think about.

Ivete glanced at her mother, her neck stretched as she looked out the window, her fingers working her now empty ring finger. Just a few weeks ago, her mother took care to shield Ivete from the truth of the world. Now she was using it as ammunition to teach Ivete that she knew nothing of the real world. To make Ivete promise not to do any damage to her relationship with Henry, at least not until they'd returned from Montana.

Now, her mother was ripping down all her carefully placed ideals. One after another. Henry is this. Your father does that. Even your brothers. Were there no good men? Was such a thing pure fiction? Were the authors of these books so creative to veer so far from reality?

Yet, her mother loved her father. Ivete saw it in their relationship, in the way her mother rubbed the pale strip that marked where her ring should be.

Ivete reached out a hand to calm her mother. "I'm sorry he took your wedding ring."

Mother flattened her hands on her skirt to stop her fidgeting. "It wasn't my original, you know. Your father thought I should have a larger stone. Maybe he'll finally see the risk in such displays of wealth."

Ivete nodded. Her parents had married for love, but their story also lacked the romance Ivete had read about. Ivete's mother allowed her husband dalliances, expected them even. And she could not envision how Ivete's own marriage might be any different. She assumed Ivete, too, would marry a man who amused oneself at the club and, like her mother, would accept such behavior. Worse, she'd called her a child when Ivete tried to push against this twisted norm.

The door opened again, slamming against the wall, and her mother let out a yelp, reaching to grip Ivete's arm.

"Joe said there was a pretty one in here. C'mon." The man stared at Ivete and waved a pistol in a circular motion as though he expected her to join him at the doorway.

"I don't want to shoot your mama." He handled his gun with the distinct click of the trigger and pointed. "Come with me." He narrowed his eyes, waiting.

Ivete stood with the slow movements of a cornered rabbit.

"We've already been robbed." Ivete exposed her upturned hands, showing she had nothing of value left.

"I don't want your gold."

Mother shot to her feet. "No, you can't take her!" She slipped sideways, placing her body in front of Ivete, a paltry but determined shield. "You can't." A gulp belied her confident tone. With a swipe of his arm, the man flung Ivete's mother to the side of the car.

Her body hit the wall, rattling the car, then slid to the floor. She lifted a hand to her head, groaning.

Ivete lunged for her mother. "Mama!" Before she reached her mother, the man gripped Ivete's arm. With the strength of a laborer, he hauled her from the car, shutting the door to her mother's protests. Another man waited outside her cabin.

Her captor pulled Ivete down the corridor. "Keep her ma inside."

Her feet tripped over themselves as she attempted to keep up with him in the tight hallway. He dragged her out of the dark hallway and into the bright sun. Blinking, she almost tripped going down the steep iron steps, but as soon as her feet hit the gravelly dirt bed of the train tracks, she found her footing. He pulled her again, down a rocky slope toward a grassy clearing some yards away. She looked back at the train, a massive beast from this new perspective several feet lower than the deck she'd stood on when she boarded the train in Chicago. The passengers inside stared at her like she was an actress on a stage. Her captor passed her to a younger boy and returned to the train.

"Why am I the only one out here? Don't you usually make *all* the people get out?" Ivete's knowledge of train robberies extended to the purely fictional.

The stony-faced boy ignored her, focusing on the side of the car. For a moment, Ivete wondered if he was stupid, then her gaze locked on a tall man, come from another car further back along the tracks.

The boy fumbled with his gun, his grip pinching Ivete's arm as it tightened. "Stay back." From the tremor in his voice, Ivete assumed the approaching man was not part of their gang. She watched the man's approach with her head cocked as though she were reading the situation on a page and not living it.

"I'd be pleased if you passed my wife back to me," the man drawled, lifting his eyebrows as he made eye contact with the boy.

"I ... I can't. We're bringin' boss a pretty girl."

Ivete's eyes flew wide. For the first time since she saw the masked man riding beside the train, she felt a flicker of fear. And a great helping of naivete. Why had she ever thought this a fun game, a diversion to make up for the months of boring baby talk that lay before her? Because she was a pampered and protected lady, that's why. Nothing bad had ever happened that her daddy's money couldn't fix. Until now. They already had everything she owned of value, after all, and still they wanted more. They wanted her. Her stomach roiled. She swallowed to keep back the fear-laced bile rising in her throat. He tugged her closer again.

"Your boss's name Harder?"

The boy who clutched her arm nodded.

"Harder and I are friends." The man picked at his fingernails as though this conversation didn't determine a human's fate. "You ever talk to your boss?"

When the kid shook his head, Ivete could almost hear the hollow echo inside.

"My name's Thomas McMullin. If he gives you trouble, you drop my name. He'd be none too pleased if you brought the wife of his friend as a trophy."

The boy opened his mouth to protest, but Thomas continued.

"This is my wife. I promised our Lord that I would protect her with my life. Unless you intend to shoot me now, I must insist you pass her to me. Even a kid like you can respect a promise to the Almighty." He reached out an arm, his palm facing the sky as though he expected the kid to hand her over without any more discussion.

The boy glared at his outstretched hand. "How come you weren't with her? You came from down there." He waved his gun at the end of the train.

"I was using the facilities when the train stopped. You boys sure gave us a shock. Been trying to get back to her ever since."

The boy scrutinized Ivete's face. "She isn't glad to see you."

Ivete winced and her lip quivered at her mistake.

Thomas's face turned comical. "No, she wouldn't be. She's too innocent to understand exactly why you have her, and at the moment, she is angry with me. You see, we just purchased a few horses, and she wanted a Dappled Gray for herself. I knew she would not appreciate such coloring once it faded and instead bought her a Bay. Now, however, your friends are taking *all* my horses, and the argument is moot. Darling." He curled his fingers as though commanding her to his side.

The boy tightened his hold and cast a dark eye at Ivete. The moment the boy's gaze was on her, Thomas reached out with the swiftness of a snake and pulled Ivete into his arms. The boy's hand burned Ivete's arm as it lost in the tug-of-war with Thomas McMullin. He trained his gun on the man, moving it between Thomas and Ivete as though unsure who to shoot first.

"I thank you for allowing me to escort my wife back to our cabin. I'm sure my gallant bravery will earn her forgiveness." He tucked her slightly behind him and along his side.

Ivete nodded, reaching up to take his hand in hers. He smiled at her like a moon- eyed schoolboy. This close up, Mr. Thomas McMullin—hero and, apparently, actor extraordinaire—made her feel a bit dizzy. He was *too* everything. His face too handsome, his eyes too green, his jaw too hard, his lips too full, his dimples too devastating. His hold on her definitely too warm and, alarmingly, too right. He looked like he'd stepped right off the pages of one of her books, and her heart pumped too fast just looking at him. But she had work to do. She'd not yet done her bit to convince the boy they were what Mr. McMullins said they were—married. She stood on tiptoe to press her lips against his cheek, but he met her mouth, kissing her full on. Soft lips matching her own in a warm greeting. She gasped, pulled away, but he braced his large hands on her back, trapping her against him. The rake! The scoundrel! He was no hero. But... perhaps such an enthusiastic embrace was necessary to convince the boy. And it was nice. She relaxed into the kiss. The moment she began to relax, Thomas released her. She swayed slightly as he urged her behind him. Ivete was grateful the boy wouldn't see her blush. No matter how she controlled her limbs, she could not prevent the blood that heated her face.

When Ivete was shielded completely by his body, Thomas spoke. "Thank you, son. The good Lord is pleased with your choice this day. Harder will just have to find himself a whore tonight."

Though she'd escaped a fate more miserable than she dared imagine, Ivete flinched at the harsh word. His hands prodded her arms and back as he nudged her to the train and up the stairs. Ivete made for her cabin.

Thomas steered her in the opposite direction. "We can't go back there. You'll have to hide unless you want to spend the night with Aaron Harder. The rest of them will look for you once they realize what happened. A prayer for that kid's life wouldn't go amiss."

"They'd kill him?" Ivete asked, glancing over her shoulder at the man.

"She speaks." He nudged her toward the train car.

Ivete let the man prod her along in whatever direction he had planned. She'd been trained as well as any soldier on the importance of following orders, be it mother and society norms, or a rogue cowboy. As she moved, she tried to decide what she'd expected when she came west. Her corset pinched as she tried to calm her breathing. Her body hadn't yet decided she was safe from the bandits that had almost taken her. Her mind wasn't sure either, but a part of her was still curious of the whole ordeal. As though she'd longed for a western adventure like that of her books, but never really believed it was possible.

Though stress rolled off Thomas with every jerky move-ment, she couldn't suppress the small smile that flattened her mouth. Could the west really be so wild, even still? Were there really charming cowboys who saved a girl from a fate more horrible than death? Suddenly this pause from Chicago, from Henry, felt like everything she needed. Perhaps an adventure in the west would prove her mother right, that in order to live as her parents lived, she needed to accept the flaws that accompanied their lifestyle. Or maybe, instead of living with her nose in a book she could live an adventure of her own.

2

They rushed through car after car. When they reached a dining car with several guests spread out at the elegant round dining tables, Thomas murmured, "Here." He came to her side, his arm brushing her shoulder.

She stopped and looked up at him. Was that fear in his eyes? Ivete brushed away all thoughts of adventure and scanned the space for a spot to hide.

Thomas raised a knowing brow at the passengers. "We were never here."

The frightened guests nodded in compliance, though there was no way for them to be certain that this man was not her abductor. She leaned into him, finding his hand and taking it so they might understand he was a friend.

Thomas's hand closed around hers and he gestured to the corner of the room where a small butler's pantry stood. The white linen curtains hung open, but no server was in sight. Ivete understood and rushed over, Thomas's boots brushing her skirts as he followed. Ivete reached for the curtain, to tug it closed, but Thomas said, "No. If it's closed, they'll look."

Instead, he slid a wheeled drink cart from the corner and Ivete tucked herself in its place. Thomas squatted next to her, blocking her into the wall, and wheeled the drink cart as close as he was able. Once they were situated, he squatted next to her. She blinked at him in the silence until one of the other passengers spoke. "I can see your head."

Thomas winced and tried to make himself smaller, but his body wasn't flexible enough to fit in the small space he'd made. He bumped the cart and rattled the silverware, making both of them flinch.

With a huff, Ivete gathered her skirts and lifted onto her knees. She whispered, "You move into the corner. I can be on the outside and make myself smaller." He scooted over, and Ivete almost laughed at the amount of space he took up, even when trying to fold himself. He hugged his knees, but Ivete thought a small horse could fit in the space under his legs. She slid her hand between his knees and pressed them away from each other. Settling herself between his folded legs with her back to him, she pulled the wheeled cart close once more.

"How is that?" she called out to the passengers.

"Better. Just your skirt."

Ivete silently cursed the deep purple dress she'd worn. She'd chosen the high-end silk in a boutique back home because of the way it caught the light. Now, the fabric would be a beacon to anyone pursuing them. She reached for a stack of white napkins on the drink cart and arranged them along the hem of her skirt, praying they would block the bold color.

Thomas spoke from behind her. "I wish I were between you and them."

"Me too," Ivete whispered.

Long arms closed around her shoulders, like he was

folding his arms in prayer. Ivete sent a silent plea to the heavens as Thomas pulled her back into his arms as though the difference of six inches and a forearm could protect her from the men who wanted to take her away.

Her voice was tight, the heat of his embrace making her heart gallop in her chest. "Thank you for your help. If I'd known what they had in mind, I would never have left the train car."

"I doubt you'd have had much choice. You're no match for those men."

Ivete swallowed as she thought of her mother, wounded and alone in their cabin. "I've always heard in real life you give them your money, and they go on their way. Is kidnapping common?"

"More than you'd think, and you look like a plum, ripe for picking."

Heat rose in Ivete's cheeks. She'd worn her lowest cut evening dress, giving full display to her breasts and scandalizing her mother. That morning, when Ivete had dressed, she was still reeling from the injustice of a world where men did far more than reveal their necks before supper. The impropriety had been the sole reason she'd chosen the gown. The prospect of both shocked and admiring eyes was something she needed as she dealt with her fiancé's physical rejection of her. He'd never so much as *tried* anything inappropriate with Ivete. Some might be glad for his respect, but in the light of all he'd done with another, it felt more like a harsh rebuff.

She'd been a fool. No wonder she'd been hauled off the train by a dirty thief. "How did you know they'd let me go?"

"I didn't. When I saw that first man bring you out, I began counting the bullets in my belt. I knew I didn't have enough to kill the whole band, and they'd surely kill me first. It wasn't until he left you with that puppy of a kid that I knew I stood a chance."

Ivete turned to look at him, but their proximity meant the most she could see was the stubble on his chin. "Do you truly think they'll kill him?"

"Maybe." His whisper was barely a breath.

The car door banged open, shaking everything around them. Thomas tightened his arms around her, his breath hot as it traveled from her hair, down her neck. She reached both hands to grip Thomas's forearms as though clinging to the face of a cliff.

A gruff voice came from behind the curtain. "We're looking for a girl; anyone new been through here?"

Ivete shrunk closer to Thomas. The inability to see the train robber or the passenger's reactions made waiting even more terrifying. She had no idea if someone in the car was using their hands to give Ivete and Thomas away.

"We ain't seen no one since you folk came in here and took our money."

The sound of a smack echoed throughout the cabin. "Shut up."

Silence.

"Thing is, the last car saw them. Either you saw them too, or they got off before your car."

A bullet rang out from outside the train, and Ivete's breath hitched in her throat. Thomas's hand clamped over her mouth, and Ivete slapped both her hands on top of his, as though the layers of flesh could take back the sound she'd made.

The sound of a door opening and closing echoed in the silence that followed. No one in the car made a sound. Thomas didn't remove his hand from her mouth nor release his grip on her waist. She couldn't remember when it had moved below her shoulders. Shallow breaths were all Ivete allowed to pass through her nose. He loosened his grip on her mouth, but his stillness gave the impression that danger grew near, and Ivete remained tense as a deer ready to bolt.

The door opened again. "McGregor, get out here. Lark's been shot."

The door closed, and once again, the car was bathed in silence. Thomas's hand dropped from her mouth to her waist and her hands went with it.

"They're gone," a passenger's voice whispered from the other side of their hiding place. Neither Thomas nor Ivete answered but remained locked in one another's embrace. Ivete looked down to see her hands still coupled with his from when they were on her face. She lay her head against his chest, her breast heaving as panic overtook her.

"Take a deep breath." His lips were against her ear. She drew a ragged breath. "Now let it go."

Ivete's exhale was shaky, and she tried once more. Thomas slid his hands from around her waist and the urge to pull them back around her almost overpowered her. Taking his lead, she leaned away from him, creating once more the six-inch distance they'd had when they first folded themselves into their hideout.

The train lurched. They waited while the engine noise grew, and the craft crept forward. Once the pace seemed too fast for the robbers to catch them, Ivete pushed the cart away and crawled away from Thomas.

Turning to face him, she got a decent look at his face for the first time. Dark blonde eyebrows set over green eyes. His mouth was lifted on one side as he surveyed her in the same manner.

Ivete broke the stare, shaking the folds from her skirts. "My mother will be worried sick."

Thomas nodded and followed her from their hiding place, his knees cracking in protest. Once they stood in the line of sight of the other passengers, Ivete was overwhelmed with gratitude.

"Thank you," she said, scanning the group. The words weren't nearly enough for the risk they'd taken. Her gaze fell on a man with a red-stained cheek. He must have been the man who was slapped.

Her attention shifted to Thomas as he came to her side, placing a hand between her shoulders and tipping his hat at the group. "Much obliged."

Ivete wanted to say more, should say more, but with every passing second she felt her energy leave her. Now that the danger was gone, her body went from relaxed to fatigued, and she had nothing to offer them.

Thomas urged her toward the door. "Let's go find your mother." Ivete made her way down the hall on shaky legs. Thomas's strong presence loomed behind her. When they reached her cabin, she stopped and turned to him. The tight corridor lent no amount of decent space between them, but Ivete didn't want any. She wanted him close as he had been before. Wanted to reach out and gather his shirt in her fists to pull him to her again. Instead she settled for a demure smile, one her mother would be proud of in the face of her ordeal.

"Thank you."

With the same tip of his hat, he gave her a full smile before turning to go. Once he was out of sight, Ivete entered her cabin.

Her mother was kneeling on the floor and resting her head against a seat cushion. Her back shook as her cries filled the cabin.

"Mama, I'm here." Ivete collapsed on the ground next to

her mother. Her skirts hadn't even settled from the swift movement when she held her mother tight.

"Ivete?" Her mother lifted her head and looked at her as though she were a ghost. "I thought they'd taken you."

"No, Mama. I'm here."

Her mother took Ivete's face in her hands and stared into her eyes. "The West isn't for us. I don't know how your brother manages it. I suppose the only option for a wife out here is a common one. No woman with options would choose to live in this horrid place."

From terror to judgment in the blink of an eye. Impressive, even for her mother. Ivete rolled her eyes but helped her mother situate herself on the seat once again and offered a handkerchief.

"I have mine." Her mother waved away Ivete's, pulling one from her own sleeve.

Ivete settled herself back in the same seat she'd been in when the train had stopped. She looked out the window at the expanse of trees and underbrush. The scenery was exactly as it had been before the robbery. If she tried, she could pretend it never happened. Her mother could be dabbing at her eyes because Ivete was refusing to marry the man her mother had chosen for her daughter. Yet, as she looked out, her heart once again picked up it's galloping pace. She could imagine the sound of hooves as the robbers overtook the train. Feel the warmth of Thomas's arms as he crushed her to him. The press of his lips against hers. No, nothing was the same.

WHEN THE TRAIN stopped in Billings, Ivete and her mother disembarked with a collective sigh of relief. Ivete couldn't stop her eyes from roving the throng for Thomas's sandy hair.

"Who are you looking for?" Mother leaned in. Her ear brushed Ivete's as though trying to follow her daughter's gaze.

"Just surveying the area. I can't believe Bastien lives out here. It's practically the wild west." Her words were true. The building fronts bore chipped paint and tobacco spittoons lay to the side of the entrances. The men that moved along the station's deck wore frontier hats with wide rims and a dip in the center rather than the more fashionable bowlers or classic toppers.

After being directed by the station master, Ivete and her mother set off for the hotel. passing horses and wagons instead of buggies and cobblestoned streets. Bastien hadn't been clear who would be picking them up, only where they should stay upon their arrival.

"We are Maxine and Ivete Graham. There should be accommodations." Her mother's self-assured attitude turned the question into a statement.

The man led them to their room while informing them of the schedule for meals.

When they were alone, her mother let out a huff as she sat on the bed. "That was more than an adventure. I think I will wire your father now and tell him what happened. He must come to collect us. I'll not ride a train alone again in my life."

"Mother, what would Papa have done? Those men had guns. Would you like him to get killed?"

"Of course not, but I can't imagine what would have happened if they'd taken you."

Warmth bloomed in Ivete's chest as she recalled her mother's courage when the man came for Ivete. "You were brave, Mama." She sat next to her mother and wrapped an arm around her shoulders.

Her mother let out a chuckle and laid her head on Ivete's shoulder. "I understand you didn't like what I was saying on the train. About Henry." She twisted to look at Ivete. "Not six months ago, you wanted Henry so badly you were in tears. Telling your father and I that we should allow you to wed before twenty-one. Now you're going to throw it all away. I want you to think about what you're doing. Not everyone marries for love."

"You did." Ivete brushed a lock of hair from her mother's face.

"Yes, and that didn't stop him from frequenting those clubs you so loathe. I didn't tell you that to ruin him in your eyes. Only so you might make a well-informed decision. Instead of one based on the tales in one of your books."

Ivete's stomach dropped at the topic that kept creeping in every conversation between her and her mother. *My own father is as bad as Henry.* She closed her eyes.

Mother's voice was light, ever the one to bounce back from defeat. "I'm going to the post office. Would you like to come along?"

"No." Ivete pinched the bridge of her nose. "My head hurts."

"You've had a big day." Her mother's voice quivered, but not with fear. Ivete could almost hear her telling this story to her friends back home. She would be animated, with her hands flying around the air as she described the scene.

Once alone, Ivete leaned back on the pillows and stared at the beamed ceiling. The way the cushions curved around her reminded her of Thomas's embrace. Henry had never held her that way, but he'd never had cause. Maybe if he'd been on the train with them, he would have done the same.

Though, Ivete had to admit that Thomas's soothing words proved he was one well-versed in the wiles of the west. Something that Henry, with all his money and silk ties, could never claim.

But she'd seen Thomas's distress. He might have a way with words, but the west was not to be tamed. Unlike Henry, whose smooth speech and family money meant that everything in his life went to plan. Even now, he expected Ivete to overcome her encounter with his fancy woman. Everyone expected it, from her friends to her own parents. Yet, Bastien had found his way out here, away from expectation and lived among such danger and uncertainty.

3

The bell above the door clanged as Thomas stepped through the post office door. A woman stood at the counter. She was finishing a wire message, and from the number of coins she was stacking on the counter, the letter had been a lengthy one.

"I can help you here, sir," a young woman offered as she made her way from the storeroom.

Thomas stepped forward from his place in line.

He gave a polite smile to the woman. "Anything for Thomas McMullin?"

The woman slid a list in front of her and adjusted her glasses, searching the names. When she shook her head Thomas took a breath. "All right. I need to send a wire to Bastien Graham in Aster Ridge. I'd like a runner to take it out to his—"

"Excuse me, sir," the woman with the coins cut in. She stretched her neck as she surveyed him with lowered brows. "Did you say Bastien Graham?"

"Yes." Thomas tried to place this woman who recognized him.

"Bastien Graham is my son. Are you acquainted?"

"We are. Are you Maxine Graham?" He glanced around. There had been word of a sister as well.

"I am." Her maternal pride shone through her voice.

"Well, that's easy. I was just going to send him a wire to see if I might be of service in bringing you back to Aster Ridge. He said his sister would be here as well."

"She's at the hotel. Our train was robbed, and she is still recovering from the ordeal."

Thomas tried not to roll his eyes at stuffy women fainting over a robbery. It was women like the one he'd rescued who had a concrete reason to complain. He pushed her from his mind. A woman with the kind of money to afford her cabin would have nothing to do with a laborer like himself.

"I was on the same train, ma'am. Afraid my horses were stolen. I was going to send a note to Bastien. Inform him of our time frame, then see about acquiring a horse and wagon. You two are at The Sheridan?"

Her face fell. "Oh." Her voice sounded stark. It even trembled. "We thought Bastien himself would escort us."

Thomas bit back a laugh. "Once we learned I would be in Billings at the same time, he gave me all the information to get you ladies home. Allow me to arrange horses and a wagon for the journey, and I'll meet you at The Sheridan in an hour. You can let me know when you will be ready to leave for Aster Ridge."

Once out of the woman's presence, Thomas drew a lungful of air. Her clothing and her voice had told him enough. Years of being looked down upon by rich folk had taught him well. Stay down. Stay quiet. The prospect of taking her and her daughter to Aster Ridge made his shoulders tense. He hadn't realized Bastien's family was so wealthy. The man had a large ranch and plenty of animals, yet he spent his days working alongside Thomas, with the sun on his face in the summer and the snow on his shoulders in winter.

Billings was a bustling town filled with folk from all over the territory and beyond. Purchasing a horse and wagon was as easy as walking into a stable and handing over the money. He arrived at the hotel half an hour before Mrs. Graham would be expecting him. He stepped into the foyer and took a seat on one of the plush chairs. He had yet to find accommodations for tonight, but there was no way he'd spend the money to stay in this place, not when a large portion of he and Bastien's business had just been stolen. He shook his head at the manifest he'd been urged to fill out regarding his stolen property. The idea that he'd get his horses back was absurd. It wasn't as though the mares had wandered off. Those bandits were as likely to return the mares as Thomas was likely to hold that woman in his arms again.

He slid his eyes to the doors that led to the bar, imagining a tall glass of the Cuban rum they kept on the high shelf.

"Thomas?" a voice came from his right. He jerked his head around. Ivete stood in her shimmering plum dress that demanded attention. The color set off her dark auburn hair and fair skin. When his eyes reached her face once more, her head was cocked as she surveyed him with amusement on her lips.

"You?" He huffed at the impossibility of her showing up like this. Then a smile played on his lips. Of course, she was here. This was the most expensive hotel in Billings. "Are you yet recovered from your adventure?"

She sat in the armchair next to his, arranging her skirts. "Quite. In fact, I found I didn't need the rest I so craved. Now

I've had a taste of adventure, as you say, I realize it is quite invigorating."

Thomas laughed. "When all turns out." A young girl like her need not realize how close she came to trauma and ruin. "Now I have spoiled you. You'll think it is safe to ride the train all over the Territories."

She played with the folds in her dress. "I do not wish to experience any bit of that again. My mother is sending a letter to my father now. He will be escorting us on the trip home, though maybe we should hire you instead." She met his eyes. "You have a lot of experience with bandits?"

"More than some."

The tall figure of Maxine Graham caught his eye as she approached. Thomas stood, prepared to take his leave of this beauty and deal with business.

Maxine met him with a smile. "I see you have met my daughter." Her gaze slid to the young woman and back to Thomas. "How soon can we leave?"

He looked between the two women. "Daughter?"

"My daughter, Ivete." Maxine's chest puffed as she gave her daughter a tight-lipped smile.

"What is going on?" Ivete cut in, scooting to perch on the edge of her seat.

Understanding came together like cards in a deck. "I work with your brother. I'm to accompany you two to his ranch in Aster Ridge." He turned his attention to Maxine. "We can leave first thing in the morning if you'd like."

Ivete stood, demanding his attention once more. "You know Bastien?"

Thomas nodded. "And Della."

Maxine ignored their exchange and pressed ahead. "First thing in the morning is best. I don't want to come all this way just to miss the birth." Maxine stepped closer and looked down at Ivete. "Shall we take dinner in our room?"

Ivete gave her mother a loaded look, her eyes flicking in Thomas's direction. "We must invite Thomas to eat with us, Mother. He is the man who saved me from those filthy men."

Maxine looked down her nose at Thomas as though doubting her daughter's claims. "You never told me that."

Thomas bounced his knee at Maxine's scrutiny. "I didn't know she was Bastien's sister, but I'm happy to have helped. No meal necessary. I was only here to discuss our departure." He stood. "I'll return in the morning, and we can set off." His fingers brushed the brim of his hat and he made his way to the exit.

He stepped into the first bar he found and ordered cheaper rum than was his usual. The burn served to remind his body of its place.

THE NEXT MORNING he parked the wagon in front of The Sheridan with two saddled mares in tow. They were inferior to the beasts he'd loaded onto the train yesterday but would provide the women with an option when the jolting of the wagon became too much to bear.

Thomas had loaded the last of the items into the wagon when Ivete made her appearance, this time adorned in a gown as blue as the wide Montana sky. He crouched, giving a buckle on the saddle more attention than necessary, afraid to get caught staring. Though she wasn't in his sight, he thought of the way her azure dress made her gray eyes glow a startling blue. He tried to brush the memory from his mind but he kept recalling the way they had raked his face in the moment of safety after hiding in that butler's pantry.

Thomas adjusted the stirrups on one of the new horses. Thank goodness his saddles and supplies had not been stolen from the train when his horses were. His gear, combined with the women's trunks, were all that filled the wagon. Maxine opted to ride in the wagon with Thomas, while Ivete chose a horse.

As they traveled west, Thomas hardly noticed the scenery. He'd lived his whole life in this open prairie that ended only when the trees began and went on for thousands of acres. First lived, then worked on different farms, lending a hand to tend horses or run cattle. All the while saving for a ranch of his own. As he drove, he kept the wagon to the grassy roads. The trees held danger, be it wildlife or more of Aaron's men looking to take their purse.

Their slower pace meant the sun dipped below the horizon before they reached their hotel. Outside the city, accommodations were basic, nothing like The Sheridan. Thomas eyed Maxine as they unloaded.

She placed her hands on her lower back and stretched. "I'll be glad for a hot meal. I wager I'll sleep like a babe tonight."

"You should have ridden with me." Ivete looked at the dusky town. She imagined even in full daylight the storefronts would be just as drab.

Maxine gestured for Thomas to take one of their smaller trunks, and the group entered the hotel. The manager led them to Ivete and Maxine's room, and Thomas set down the trunk inside the door.

"Would you like anything else from the wagon?" he asked Maxine, unsure whether he should speak to Ivete or not. She'd kept her distance the whole day. At first, Thomas thought she'd suffer from riding so long, but her bright eyes said otherwise.

Maxine smiled. "That is all. Thank you, Thomas." She turned her back on him with a wave of her hand, the exact movement she'd used when dismissing the hotel clerk earlier. A dismissal, clear and simple. Thomas left the room for his quarters.

As Thomas settled into his room, he sagged into a chair, fatigued from the long day of leading the wagon. Yet the image of the beautiful Ivete alongside him on a horse lifted his spirits. It was no wonder Harder's men had chosen her. For a moment, he questioned his refusal to join Harder all those years ago. Not for access to unwilling maids, but because the money was quick and he might have set himself up with a ranch of his own by now. He might be able to offer such a woman something besides callused hands and dirty boots. Years ago he'd traded in easy access to rich bounties for hard work and blisters. Neither prevented him from returning to Bastien empty-handed.

Rather than turn in for the night, Thomas shook thoughts of Ivete from his mind and made his way to the bar to beg a drink. The moment the glass touched his lips, a woman in a red and black dress approached.

"What's a feller like you doin' all alone?"

Thomas glared at the woman and took another sip.

"And so ornery too. How about I give you something to smile about." She leaned in and pressed herself against Thomas's side.

"No, thanks," Thomas grumbled. Though, with his mind so full of Ivete, he was almost tempted. The woman in red didn't give up. She prodded Thomas with questions about ranch life, as though she were interested. He threw back the rest of his rum, wincing as it burned its way down, and gave the woman a nod before retreating to the safety of his room where his only choices were which side of the bed to sleep.

Though the day had been tiring, he lay with his hands behind his head as thoughts swirled in his mind. He'd rejected the barroom lady, but she was a realistic option. Ivete, in her fancy silks, should not even be on his mind. He should consider her like any other bit of gear being shuffled from the train station to the ranch. She was as much his as the saddles in the wagon. He worked for Bastien; everything he was hauling belonged to that man, and Thomas wouldn't do anything to cross his employer. Not when he was so close to the funds he needed to buy a ranch of his own.

4

_____

Ivete's body cried out from the strain of yesterday's ride, and she'd been loath to lace herself into her corset this morning. But she'd done it. With a groan or two. And over it, she'd pulled on her plainest dress. The room where they'd slept had grubby windows and more than dust in the corners of the floorboards. No use ruining her finest with the dust of the road, even if it did mean arriving in Aster Ridge and meeting her new sister-in-law looking like a well-worn dish rag. "Come," Ivete's mother demanded, before bustling into the hall.

Ivete took one last look around the room in search of anything left behind before closing the door.

In the hallway, she narrowly avoided bumping into a woman. The woman bore rouge stained cheeks and unnaturally pink lips. Ivete flushed and turned her eyes down. The woman's dress was red with black lace, her shoes in desperate need of a polish.

"Pardon me." The woman swept around Ivete and down the stairs.

Ivete watched the woman. This was likely what Henry's

club was like— painted women roaming freely between sunlit barrooms and moonlit bedrooms, trailing smiling gentlemen behind them like eager pups. The woman didn't spare Ivete a second glance, but Ivete could not look away. This was a woman like Henry's lover and Ivete watched in awe at how the woman floated down the stairs, all swaying hips, then leaned close to the manager for a muffled conversation.

Ivete tried, but was unable to muster the disdain her mother had expressed for this type of woman. Instead, Ivete sent up a silent prayer that this woman would never experience the heartbreak experienced by Henry's mistress. Her thoughts accompanied her down the stairs and out onto the boardwalk. Her mother waited near the wagon. Ivete shook the troublesome thoughts away and focused on more manageable problems. "My legs are quite sore. I'm going to ask Thomas to arrange a seat in the wagon. You can ride up top." She nodded toward the seat on the springs.

"Oh, nonsense. I'll ride for a bit this morning. I'm sure my back will appreciate a varied day. It is still angry with me for yesterday." Her mother rubbed her spine as she broke away from Ivete to check her saddle.

The woman wearing the red and black dress exited a side door of the hotel and stopped short when she saw Thomas. The two shared a smile and a nod before she continued on her way.

Ivete closed her eyes and bit her lips, a burst of heat crushing her chest. Her mother was right. All men did these things. If that were true, marrying rich was the wisest choice. Ivete swallowed her pride and approached Thomas.

He lifted his gaze when Ivete drew near. No wonder he'd been so talented in kissing. No wonder his touch had been so strong, steady, and perfect. Ivete was hardly the first woman he'd touched. His smiling exchange with the woman in red made that clear. Thomas was an expert in such matters because he had plenty of experience. She flushed. His kisses. His touch. She was naive to have let them impact her so.

One side of his mouth lifted in a cocky smile. "Good morning."

Ivete narrowed her eyes at this rogue groom of Bastien's who had saved her from an uncertain fate. The grooms in Chicago didn't stare so openly nor have such straight teeth and strong jawlines. She met his eyes, challenging his brazen stare. "I'll be riding in the wagon this morning." Ivete lifted her skirts and made to climb up the wagon.

With boldness no groom should possess, he took her waist and hauled her up, so her feet found the toe board. She pivoted and sank onto the wooden board. The seat and well-worn springs gave a few hearty bounces.

Thomas grinned at her. "The wagon is old, but those springs are none the worse for it." He worked on tying down a canvas that covered the supplies.

"Are you expecting poor weather?"

He didn't take his eyes from the job. "This is Montana, miss. I always expect rain."

Her mother rode her horse around the wagon.

"You look good up there, Mother. I haven't seen you ride in years."

"Nonsense. I've ridden."

Ivete pursed her lips. If the woman had ridden in recent memory, Ivete had certainly not been witness to the event. No use correcting her, though.

Thomas rubbed his hands together and ran a critical eye over the wagon and horses. With a curt nod, he climbed into the seat next to Ivete, their arms brushing.

He snapped the reins, and Ivete gripped the side of the seat when the horses lurched forward.

"So what is it my brother does out here? You said horses were stolen, but I thought he raised cattle."

Thomas kept his eyes forward as he spoke. "He does both. Plenty of land for cattle to graze, but I think breeding horses is where his heart is."

Ivete chewed on this bit of information. Where was her heart? The further she got from Henry, the less she felt it belonged to him. And yet, what else was there for a woman? She glanced at her mother. A woman not only content, but happy with her life. Would Ivete ever be able to find contentment? Or was she to forever push against what others told her would make her happy?

As the day wore on, Ivete wondered why wagons weren't built with better seats, ones with backs to lean against, possibly a few cushions.

Ivete pressed her fist into the base of her back. "Now I know why Mother was aching this morning. Do you hurt?"

"A bit. I guess I'm used to it."

Ivete gave him a quizzical look. "You're used to pain?"

He laughed. "Riding might help." He jerked his chin toward the saddled horse he'd tethered to the back of the wagon.

She shook her head. "My legs are still aching from yesterday."

Silence fell over them once again, and she surveyed Thomas's profile as he studied the road ahead. His hair was the color of wheat, and his nose had a small bump as though it had been broken.

He must have felt her gaze because his eyes slid sideways before he swiveled to fully face her. He lifted his eyebrows. "Yes?"

Ivete drew back, but couldn't turn her eyes from him as heat flooded her cheeks. "I was wondering; do you often save women from your robber friend?"

He barked a laugh and looked forward again. "I try to keep it to three times a week."

"Do you always escort the women home afterward?" Ivete's smile fell as her ill-thought words took on a new meaning. The woman from the hotel flashed into her mind. "I didn't mean ... I only meant how you're taking me to Bastien now."

A smile split his face, and tiny lines crinkled at the corner of his eyes.

"No offense taken, ma'am." He flicked his gaze at her as if assuring her that her words did not hurt him. "I've never saved anyone before. I rarely ride the train, and after that, I doubt I'll be riding one again. At least not with any important cargo."

"Like horses or a wife?"

He laughed. "Like horses or a wife."

"You were quite brave. Saving me. How do you know the gang leader? What if it hadn't been your friend's men?"

"Then I suppose you and I wouldn't be having this conversation."

"Hmmm." Ivete shivered. The sequence of events might have been much different if Thomas hadn't been there. "Bastien will have to forgive you for losing his horses." Her stomach clenched. But her brother was unlikely to forgive Thomas for the kiss, no matter how good Thomas's motivations. "But I ask that you keep your method of saving me between the two of us."

"Absolutely." He pressed his lips into a thin line.

"Are you going to tell me how you know bandits, or am I to assume you were one yourself?"

"I was never a bandit."

Ivete waited, tilting her head and leaning forward so he could see her looking at him.

"When I left home about eight years ago, I was with my best friend, Aaron Harder. We met up with some bandits along the road. When they learned we had nothing to steal, they let us travel with them for a few days before we reached our destination. Once it was time to part ways, they offered to let us join their band. Aaron stayed. I didn't."

"And you haven't seen him since?" Ivete imagined the heartbreak if her best friend Angelica ran away with bandits, never to return.

His face fell. "I've seen him, but I'd be glad to never have to again."

"Truly? Your best friend?"

"Eight years is a long time. And in that time, he has become someone I don't recognize. If his mama knew he'd tried to have you kidnapped for his pleasure ..." He gave a slow shake of his head.

"But he would never harm *you*. You're his best friend." Ivete's eyebrows knit together as she tried to understand.

"Maybe not, but he's tried more than once to bring me into his crew. Says the money is better than anything I'm making honest." His chest rose and fell with a sigh. "The more I see him, the more chance I have of offending him with my refusal."

She supposed a man with no morals might be offended by those who had them. Yet, society had no problem allowing Henry to toss morals aside. Who was the great judge telling the world what morals were to be kept and which ones were fluid?

Ivete looked at him again. "What is it about robbery as a profession that is so unthinkable to you?"

His breath left him in a whoosh, and he swiveled his head around to stare at her. When she didn't speak, he spluttered a response. "It's dishonest. It can change the victim's life from surviving to starving. People get killed. I could be hanged." He gestured wildly with his hands and the wagon veered left. He turned back and straightened out the team. "Is that reason enough, or are you still considering a life with Aaron Harder?"

Ivete didn't deign to reply, but waited for him to go on. This topic had him talking and was a distraction from her aches. He spoke of honesty, yet he was familiar with that woman at the hotel, which placed him in the same category as Henry: men who freely used women for their pleasure. "Are you afraid your friend will hang?"

He gave a hard laugh. "Harder will hang. It's only a matter of time."

Ivete touched his forearm. "I'm sorry."

His gaze moved from where her hand lay on his arm to her face. "You wouldn't be sorry if you'd been taken. If that had happened, I daresay your brother and likely myself would hang as well."

His mention of Bastien took the wind from her lungs. "What does Bastien have to do with Harder?"

"If Harder had you, who do you think would come to snatch you from the snake pit?" He stopped and blew through his lips. "I'm just glad that kid handed you over."

Despite his words, Ivete couldn't imagine Bastien rescuing her. That role already belonged to someone, and his sandy hair curled around the brim of his wide cowboy's hat. "My father should give you some sort of payment for your actions. I'll write to him the moment we arrive."

Thomas shook his head. "Please, don't."

"Does money not excite you?"

A small smile lifted the side of his mouth. "I wasn't thinking about money." He looked at her with a twinkle in his eyes. "I was thinking about you telling your father what, exactly, I did to remove you from the situation." He lifted an eyebrow. "How you kissed me in an attempt to convince—"

Ivete placed a hand over his mouth. "Okay, okay." Her eyes flicked to her mother, far enough ahead as to not over-hear their conversation. She let her hand fall from his face but narrowed her eyes at him. "I didn't ... *you* kissed *me*."

Thomas let out a booming laugh, causing her mother to throw a glance over her shoulder.

Ivete lowered her voice. "You claimed to be an honest man, but you would use this against me?" She gulped at the image of Bastien's face if this man were to tell her brother everything. The tale didn't need much embellishing to be humiliating.

Thomas sobered and lowered his eyebrows. "I would never try to hurt you or Bastien."

Satisfied, Ivete spun in her seat so her knees faced forward again. Not until she moved away did she realize how her pleading had drawn her closer to him. Even still, the entire length of her body ran along his. From hip to shoulder they brushed against one another.

Ivete suppressed a shiver. "I think I'll ride the next time we stop."

"That would be good." His face looked pained, a contrast to his consent.

DARKNESS HAD FALLEN by the time they reached Bastien's yard. The sides of the house were a light color, and it glowed a chalky blue in the night with soft yellow candlelight coming from the windows. Before they stopped, she noticed her brother's tall frame stepping from the warm glow of the house and into the moonlight. He jogged toward them and reached up to help her dismount. "Evie." He pulled her close for a tight hug. He kept one arm around her as he faced the wagon and it's leader. "Thank you, Thomas, for delivering my family to me." He released Ivete and walked around the wagon to help their mother down. He embraced her, and their mother touched his face and hair. Ivete could not hear the quiet voices they used, but the sight warmed her heart all the same. They missed Bastien in Chicago and she drew a lungful of the crisp air, glad to finally be here, to be with her brother whom she'd missed greatly.

Thomas appeared, only half of his face lit by the moon. "I can take your horse."

Ivete studied his silhouette as she passed him the reins. She cleared her throat trying to make out the unease she felt at his transfer from companion and guardian, to stable worker. At least he hadn't called her *miss*. "You must be at least as tired as we are."

"The prospect of sleep has rejuvenated me enough to finish my duties."

Though he'd turned and his face was bathed in black, Ivete could imagine his teasing smile. "Thank you. For the train, and for bringing us safely here." Though the journey had been but two days, a deep satisfaction warmed her core as though she'd been traveling for years to reach this spot.

5

Thomas lifted the saddle off one of the horses when he heard the crunch of boots on hay.

Bastien let out a deep sigh. "Took the mares, huh?"

Thomas gave a sad nod. "I figure we should be exempt from taxes for a while. The government isn't doing enough, and I swear the train employees were expecting to stop. Did Ivete tell you they tried to take her?"

Bastien's eyes turned wild. Guess not. "What? How did she ...?"

"We were lucky it was Harder's gang." Thomas shook his head at the term *luck* used to describe losing their broodmares and almost getting shot.

"Harder ... your old friend?"

Thomas nodded, and unsaddled Maxine's mare. "They got her off the train. But once I knew they took her for Harder, I went after her."

A hand landed on his shoulder. "I am in your debt. If they'd gotten her ... How did you know who she was?"

"I didn't know. Didn't think to ask first."

Bastien laughed. "Of course. I didn't mean to imply that

you wouldn't have done that for anyone. Just a darn good coincidence."

Thomas led the horse into a stall and heaped some oats into the bucket before closing the door.

Bastien's voice was tentative when he spoke. "We lost another cow while you were away."

The words hit his chest and pressed down. Thomas had found two other dead cows in the pasture in the months before his trip to acquire new mares.

Thomas met Bastien's gaze. "All the more reason we could have used those three mares. What do you want to do?"

Bastien was the money behind their operation, and Thomas worked to earn himself half of the spring colts. Without the mares, there was no breeding or inheritance.

"I guess we buy more." Bastien chewed his lip. "No sense in waiting for Harder to return what he's stolen. I don't think he likes you *that* much."

Thomas gave a hard laugh. "Not *those* mares." He shook his head. He'd paid more than they had planned because the horses were racing stock and an excellent price for the quality. "You would have loved them." Thomas heaved a sigh, one of many since he'd lost the horses.

"Maybe now he's got a decent set of mares, your old friend will start a breeding business of his own. Make an honest living." Bastien clapped him on the shoulder. "Let's put these beasts to bed, and you can help me bring in the trunks."

Aaron Harder wouldn't start an honest trade. If he'd intended that, he would have continued on with Thomas all those years ago. No, Aaron would live high until the law cut him down for good. The thought pressed at Thomas's heart. Aaron had been like a brother to him and like any brother, it didn't matter how much of an inconvenience he was. What mattered was that he was alive. Maybe Thomas was a fool, but he'd always hoped Aaron would find his way out of the gang. But Wanted posters were in every post office and hotel from here to Kansas City. Aaron Harder was well and truly an outlaw now. The time for finding himself had passed. The best Thomas could do for his old friend was to bury him when the time came, or buy a headstone if he was too late.

———

IVETE ROLLED OVER IN BED, the stiff sheets rustling beneath her. Light filtered through the sheer curtains, beckoning her to the day ahead. When she lifted her head, she dropped it again with a groan. The two-day ride had caused her muscles to seize such that even a full night's rest couldn't force them to relax.

She dressed, every movement painful, and followed the sound of voices down the hallway and into the kitchen. Bastien and Della's home had not a single stair, so unlike their family's three-story mansion in Chicago. Instead of stacked floors, Bastien's house was a sprawling maze filled with long hallways and sunlit rooms. Here, where land was practically free, there was no need for stairs when one could spread his house as wide as one liked. As she entered the kitchen, she saw Della, her hands white with flour.

"I was just about to wake you," her mother said when Ivete approached.

"I slept like the dead. It is utterly quiet out here." She lowered herself into the chair next to her mother, both women facing Della, who worked in the kitchen, her pregnant belly sliding along the counter as she pushed and kneaded a lump of dough.

"I was just telling Della that this work is much too exhausting for her. She's going to need to hire help once the baby comes. She may as well hire it now and put up her feet."

Ivete's eyes flashed to Della, wondering how she was taking mother's demands. Most women would be glad for a staff, but Della remained an enigma to the Graham family. She'd rolled her sleeves back, and the muscles in her arms flexed in the most unladylike way with every turn of the dough. *Is it possible she likes working so hard?* A firm word from her mother told Ivete her face showed her confusion. She wiped the look and gave her mother a prim smile.

"How are my ladies?" Bastien's deep voice boomed from behind the wall along the entry. He stepped around the corner.

Before greeting Ivete or their mother, he took Della into his arms and planted a kiss on her mouth. Her giant stomach didn't deter him in the least. A stab of jealousy ripped through Ivete. Bastien was of the same class as Henry, yet something deep inside told her he was faithful to his wife. Their mother would probably claim it was because there were no other women for miles.

Before Ivete could ruminate for too long, Bastien lifted her from her chair and planted a kiss on the top of her head. "You are as beautiful as ever, dear sister. Henry is a very lucky gentleman. Are you certain he deserves you?"

Her mother cut her a silencing look before stepping between her children and accepting Bastien's embrace.

He turned and went back into the kitchen, leaning over Della to steal a hot biscuit from the tray still hot from the oven. "Two weddings in one year, Mama. You must be glad for a month in the country."

Their mother sat once more. "I'll be glad to meet my first grandchild."

He glanced at Ivete. "Would you like a ride this morning? Della's mare is underworked as of late." He ran his gaze over her attire, "Did you bring riding clothes? If not, your travel clothes will do. You aren't the belle of Chicago society out here. Just another girl on the range." He bit into the biscuit, steam rising from the hot pastry.

Ivete rolled her shoulders. Maybe a ride would loosen her strained muscles. "Yes, I brought my habit. Isn't that all you cowboys do out here, ride horses?"

Bastien laughed through his full mouth. "You've read too many dime novels. First breakfast. My wife makes food even better than Chef."

She looked sidelong at Bastien. Her brothers had always teased her about her reading. They never understood how she could read for such long stretches nor did they approve of her topic. Yet, Bastien was now living in the very world most of her books were set in. With his very own stable and farm hand. The thought of Thomas warmed Ivete's cheeks. She had yet to understand Bastien and Thomas's working relationship. Her brother had gone out to help Thomas yesterday, yet the man wasn't eating with them this morning. If he was more servant than partner, Ivete could expect him when they readied for a ride. She bit her lip to keep back the smile that threatened to reveal her thoughts.

After a breakfast that lived up to expectation, Ivete followed Bastien to the stable. Her plum riding habit swished over the tall grasses as they made their way.

"My baby sister, all grown up and getting married ..." Bastien spoke in a mock-dreamy voice.

As they entered the darkened interior of the stables, Ivete recalled the silencing look her mother had given her this morning. A surge of anger rolled through her, collecting every crumb of propriety and forced smiles over the years.

She thought of Bastien, out here in the West with a common wife and no servants. A sudden bitterness at her brother's freedom overtook her. All her pent up rage at the society they'd come from burst from her spirit. "I'm not marrying him. The wedding is off, and believe me, I don't need anyone else in my ear telling me to change my mind."

Ivete studied Bastien's startled but appraising look. What did he think? Would he disapprove, too?

A stall down the aisle slammed closed. Thomas approached and heat rose up Ivete's neck. Had he heard her outburst?

Bastien shifted his gaze from Ivete to Thomas. "We were just heading out on a ride. Care to join us?"

With great effort, Ivete stopped her jaw from dropping. A servant with them on a ride was inappropriate.

Thomas shook his head. "Got too much to do around here." He switched his gaze to Ivete, his beautiful eyes roving her face before he turned and walked past her.

Ivete's breath hitched at his inspection, and she steadied her racing heart as his long stride put distance between them.

Bastien and Ivete readied their horses. Growing up, their father had required they all be able to saddle their own, but Ivete hadn't done it in quite some time.

Bastien laughed outright at her shoddy work and tightened the girth himself.

As Thomas carried on with his morning chores, he couldn't brush away thoughts of what Ivete had said to her brother before they noticed Thomas was there. She wasn't engaged after all. A small smile graced his lips as he recalled her instant discomposure once he made his presence clear. He shook his head. He had no business thinking of her in any way besides as the sister to his employer. Thomas didn't need a full understanding of Bastien's finances to be certain that his sister was too rich for Thomas's blood. If Thomas had the potential to make a woman like her content, it wouldn't be any time soon.

Unbidden, thoughts of a girl back home came to his mind. Missy Jones, the prettiest girl in their town, had given him her affections. Even talked about marrying him. When Thomas let their secret slip to his best friend, he'd learned the worst. Aaron had been given the same promises as Thomas. She'd been playing them both. When confronted, she'd laughed and told Thomas she would never marry someone without money. He winced to think what she'd told Aaron, whose father had abandoned them years before.

Thomas's family wasn't poor. In fact, ever since his stepmother arrived, his father had grown richer as she turned his farm into a pack animal business to assist those venturing into the Yellowstone region. Nevertheless, Thomas hadn't amounted to enough for Missy Jones, and he certainly wouldn't be enough for a girl such as Ivete Graham.

He huffed a bitter laugh. He did tend to fall for rich

women, didn't he? His savings, combined with Bastien's offer for their year-long agreement, meant he would be quite comfortable when the year was over. He would be able to set up a ranch of his own. A place where his siblings could all land when their step-mother cast them out. He thought of his siblings, spread throughout Montana, spending Christmases among others and not coming together as they used to. Once he had a ranch, things would change and certainly when he was ready he could find a woman who would be happy with his circumstances.

Thoughts of the dead cows popped into his mind. Despite the large share Bastien promised, Thomas's earnings over the year were contingent upon what the ranch made as a whole. Sick cows and stolen broodmares meant the once generous agreement might turn into a waste of his time. He understood now that old cowboy song about chasing the horizon.

6

Bastien led Ivete along the borders of his extensive land. The valley was still green, though the bite in the morning air meant fall was nearly here. Wildflowers bloomed throughout the landscape, making it look like a beautiful painting, one none but a master could capture. Bastien led them up a small hill, and when they crested the rise, Ivete saw a lake below them. As they neared, Ivete noticed several ducks and a few swans.

"Swans?" Ivete raised her eyebrows. "Trying to bring a bit of home out West?"

Bastien laughed, "I thought Della would like them, but she's only been out one time. The pregnancy has been harder than either of us thought." His eyes darkened.

"Are you worried about the birth?"

He blew through his lips. "Am I ever. Della tells me women do it every day, but she's not just any woman."

"I can tell." Ivete's face relaxed as she looked out at the fowl.

"Am I allowed to ask about your nuptials? Or will you turn into a bobcat again?"

"I'm sorry." She shook her head, not knowing what else to say or how to start. "Mama would want me to tell you I am thrilled and honored to be on the cusp of blending our family with one such as the Burnhams."

"And what would *you* tell me?"

A cold wind swept through the valley, piercing the thin fabric of Ivete's riding habit. The truth stuck in her throat as a shiver ran along her arms.

"Evie." Bastien used her childhood nickname, one she hated when used by anyone except Bastien.

The memory of their younger years and the ease with which they lived each day brought tears to her eyes. "We were fortunate to live in such a family as ours. I'm not ungrateful."

Bastien nodded, moving his penetrating gaze away from her to swing off his mount and assisted her in doing the same.

"If there's anyone who understands breaking the family's expectations, it's me." He led her to a large boulder nestled in the earth, and they sat. His gaze followed a hawk gliding across the scene before them.

Ivete picked at the fabric of her wide skirts and chewed her lip. He needed to know why, and she'd tell him, but the shame that accompanied the revelation made the words stick in her throat. She straightened her spine and met her brother's eyes. "A woman approached Angelica and me in the street." She flinched, mentioning Bastien's old fiancée. Would it pain him? She searched his face. He seemed to be fine. Good. She'd not like to keep her brother and best friend separate forever. "The woman said she ... *knew* Henry." Ivete stopped, her cheeks burning at the memory. "She spat at my feet."

Bastien leaned back and let out a breath as though the comment hit him in the gut. "Jealous?"

The humiliation on the street had brought tears to her eyes, tears that threatened to return. "She and Henry knew each other in the way of husband and wife."

This comment broke Bastien's reserve and he whipped toward her. After a moment, his shock wore off, and a sly but appraising smile spread across his face. "What do you know about the ways of husband and wife?"

"I know men do these things, and wives pretend not to notice. Everything else, I learned from Angelica after she and Luc ... " Ivete's eyes flashed to Bastien. Mentioning Angelica was one thing, but mentioning her relations with Luc was quite another. Angelica and Bastien had once been intended to marry. When her friend had switched her affection to Ivete's oldest brother, Luc, Ivete feared the heartbreak Bastien would suffer upon his return from Wyoming. Instead, he'd shown up, unbroken, with a wife of his own.

Bastien and Luc's relationship had always been strained, so it was difficult to tell whether Luc's marriage to Angelica had worsened matters or whether they remained the same. Bastien had begged off attending their wedding due to Della's time being so near. But that was over a month ago. Surely, if all was well between the two brothers, Bastien could have traveled to Chicago for the wedding and returned to Aster Ridge long before the birth.

As though he read her thoughts, Bastien laughed. "You may speak of Angelica and Luc all you wish. *Please do*, to put away any of the familial gossip that may remain." He looked at her sidelong. "Though I think you and mother are the gossips. I cannot imagine Luc and Willem are inclined to discuss my feelings."

Ivete sniffed but avoided his eyes.

"Go on," he urged.

"There's not much else. I told Mother I wanted to call off the wedding. She told me I was being childish."

Bastien brushed his arm against her shoulders, leaning his head on hers. "You are young but making grown-up decisions." The stillness of the lake stretched around them. "Do *you* think you are childish?"

"I don't know. She says the wives pretend not to notice. But if nobody will talk about it, how can she be sure every husband is doing it?" Ivete drew away from him. "Is it true? Do all men do it?"

"I don't." He chuckled. Ever the jokester and never serious when she needed him to be.

"Not yet, but what about when you are older? What about when Della is no longer young and beautiful?"

"If she ever loses her beauty, I might finally be worthy of her."

"Stop making light. You two are happy now, but you won't be happy forever."

"No? And why not?" He laughed.

Ivete grit her teeth. "Because love expires. It doesn't stay on forever."

Bastien narrowed his eyes as they scanned the scene. "In the kitchen, we have a sourdough crock on the counter. All Della has to do is add a little flour and water each day, and when she's ready, it provides the yeast for making bread. Now, I assume some of the original sourdough is still there, but much of it is the flour and water from Della's daily ministrations."

"I hope you don't think baking is the answer to my problem."

"Maybe not. But my point is, some of our original love is still there, but it changes. Every day, good or bad, feeds that crock. It grows and changes. Still just as powerful and useful, but different."

Ivete wrinkled her nose. "You're becoming common. First, you invite your servant on our ride. Now you compare your marriage to some smelly old pot in the kitchen."

Bastien's laugh carried across the lake, and Ivete warmed. Her words were harsh, but he had enough confidence to laugh them away. He was her favorite brother. Willem was closest to her in age and always her tormentor. Luc never had an interest in her, not until her best friend Angelica grew into a beauty. Bastien had always been her friend, her protector against Willem. Now, he was the one person who didn't consider her mad for not wanting to marry into the Burnham family's fortune. Her heart softened as she realized he wasn't common at all, only making his own way in life.

She opened her mouth to apologize, but he spoke first. "Will it help my case if I told you Thomas isn't a servant? He does tend the livery, but only because he has an interest in the mares come spring. He and I are partnering to raise cattle on the south end of the property. Come June, he'll be off to build his own ranch. He has several siblings he'd like to care for."

Ivete tried to alter her image of him. To think of him as a business man and elder brother to his siblings. As she did so, his mossy green eyes filled her vision and she couldn't think of him as anyone except the dashing cowboy who'd saved her from train robbers, who'd held her close in his protective embrace.

Bastien broke into her daydream. "Maybe you should keep that crock metaphor between you and me. Della already teases me about my romantic abilities."

They mounted again and kept the pace slow as they made their way back to Bastien's house.

Ivete spoke into the still air. "You wouldn't marry him."

"I most definitely wouldn't. Della would be most displeased."

Ivete reached across her horse and attempted to swat her brother's arm.

Bastien laughed then bobbed his head to the side as though considering. "It depends on what you want." He glanced at her from the corner of his eye, "I hope I won't scandalize you when I tell you that Father is one of those unfaithful men Mother speaks of. It doesn't always spell unhappiness. She is right that it is accepted in their social circle. That includes Burnham."

"Yet a girl is unacceptable for marriage if she dare be alone with a man for more than a minute. It is most unfair." Ivete clenched her knees and the mare whinnied beneath her. She patted the horse softly. "Sorry about that," she grumbled.

"It certainly is. When I met Della, my eyes were opened to the struggles of womanhood. To be honest, before her, I never understood the hypocrisy even though it was in front of me my whole life. Instead, I fought against it, not exactly knowing what it was I was fighting. Eventually I gave up and left the ring. Headed for Wyoming."

Ivete heaved a sigh. Her horse mirrored her noise, prancing sideways off the path, then back to Bastien's side.

Bastien nodded toward her mount. "Dusty wants to run." *Me too.* Ivete dug her heels into Dusty's flanks, and the mare shot into the green pasture that led home. As the horse raced along, the wind whipped against Ivete's face, tangling her hair and ripping the hat from her head. Ivete slowed her mount and turned to watch in horror as Bastien's horse trampled the delicate item. He reined in his horse, dismounted, and picked up the limp accessory.

Ivete heaved a sigh. It was just as well. This was the wild west, and she had no business wearing such finery. She glanced at the hem of her habit, muddy from the walk to the lake. Who was she dressing up for, anyway? Mother? Bastien? Certainly Della didn't care what Ivete wore. And most certainly not Thomas. She hadn't even known the man when she packed for this trip. He was the last person she could be dressing for. Yet his was the face that filled her mind, and may have been the face she'd imagined when she'd chosen the plum-colored gown. Was it possible she'd hoped for her trip to be like the novels she read in the comfort of her family's drawing room back in Chicago? Had fate given her Thomas so she might have one last adventure before she settled down into the life that was expected?

7

Thomas trudged across the grass for supper at the Grahams' house. Though he ate there nearly every night, he'd tried begging off while Maxine and Ivete were visiting. His attempts had been dismissed. He now had to face the two women and swallow the guilt at having taken the guest house from them.

With a sigh, he rapped on the doorframe. Bastien called for him to enter and waved him inside.

With a deep breath, Thomas obeyed and nodded to the ladies. He couldn't find the courage to meet Ivete's eyes. That morning in the stable he had hardly been able to look away. Now his cheeks burned with shame at his unabashed stare. Her face was like a portrait, creamy white with rosebud lips. She was an artist's dream and not fit for the wiles of Montana. She would soon return to the city where a lady like her belonged.

His appearance signaled the time to gather around the dinner table. Maxine insisted on sitting next to Della. This put him next to Ivete, who had yet to utter a word of greeting. She was most certainly brushing him off for his behavior in the stable, as she well should. He would remember his place this night and for the rest of her time here.

Maxine lifted her voice, and the whole table turned their eyes to her. "I am going to take this next week to interview for a housemaid. Bastien, I cannot believe you have allowed your wife to work herself this hard."

Bastien shared a look with Della that told Thomas she didn't mind the work. "You are right, Mother. I am most wicked. Once the babe arrives, Della must have help. I suppose you two ladies are unwilling to fill in?" He scooped himself some green beans, glistening with what Thomas hoped was butter.

When Maxine scoffed at the idea, Ivete suppressed a smile.

Bastien continued, "There is no need to hold interviews. Not many girls would make it out this far anyhow. Our closest neighbors, the Morrises, have a young girl who can do the work. Their boy already makes the trek to work in the stable with Thomas and me. I'll inquire into how soon she can start."

Maxine sniffed, her nose held high. "She should start when you ask, not the other way around."

Bastien gave his mother a nod.

Thomas hoped for Eloise Morris's sake she could start right away. If she didn't Maxine might very well drag her to Aster Ridge by her ear and dock her pay before it even began. Everyone shifted uncomfortably in their seats. They may be family, but they lived life differently, that much was clear. Thomas had never liked tense silences. He searched the room for some way to break it and his gaze, unable to help itself, settled on Ivete.

"How are you liking it out here?" he asked Ivete, barely

meeting her eyes before moving them to the mashed potatoes on his plate.

"It's lovely. That pond is something to behold."

Bastien leaned forward. "Lake, Ivete. It's a lake."

She tossed her head and gave her brother a teasing smile that drew Thomas's gaze once again. He whipped it back to his plate. Safer to look there. Safer to focus on anything but her.

"Pond." Bastien chuckled to himself. "With all of us gone, there are no siblings at home to keep you in your place, Ivete." He glanced at Maxine. "Mother, I hope she's not got everyone wrapped around her little finger. We Graham brothers have spent years endeavoring to keep our sister well-rooted."

She scoffed. "Is that what you call pulling my hair and embarrassing me in front of polite company?"

Thomas risked a glance at her. She had turned to him, as if he were the polite company she spoke of. Her ivory cheeks were flushed. Bastien chortled. "I haven't pulled your hair since I was ten."

Ivete narrowed her eyes. "Maybe since *I* was ten."

Maxine sent her children a look of dismay, but her eyes held an undeniable sparkle. The room swelled with a familial bond Thomas remembered from when his own mother was alive.

His family had been larger even than Bastien's. Eleven children, all told, extra helping hands on a large and sprawling farm. But unlike many fathers, Thomas's dad wanted his children to do something different. Farming was hard labor and unpredictable. A severe rain could kill half the crop for the year. Thomas had endured years when his family could barely pay for the seed, let alone profit from their labors. Those were the early years when the mouths to feed were small. Now, through his step-mother's keen mind, his father was living a life of comfort. Many families weren't so lucky, and yet, something told Thomas his father would take back their life of labor and risk if it meant he could have his late wife back in his arms. Prosperity was all well and good, but with love, well, even on the hungriest days a man could live off of that.

After dinner, Della excused herself for an early bedtime, as she normally did. Thomas and Bastien often sat and talked business until the fire died down, but tonight, with the ladies present, they talked of more personal topics.

Ivete sat next to him, her gaze warming his cheeks. Finally, he met her eyes in the same way he'd done on the ride to Aster Ridge.

Hers narrowed in challenge. "So, did you and Bastien meet when he was in Wyoming?"

He gulped and shook his head. "We met here. He was looking for someone who knew horses. I was looking for an opportunity. Our paths crossed at the right time." Thomas glanced at Bastien, but he was conversing with his mother and couldn't come to his aid. Ivete's nearness, even her voice stirred something in him. Something that should be kept down, in its place. "How about you? Did you ever visit him in Wyoming?"

She made a noise in her throat as though the idea were preposterous. "No. That place was only temporary and, from what I heard, unsuitable for visitors."

Thomas nodded, wondering what it was about the place that made it unsuitable. He noted her clothing, from the hat that served no purpose except to set off the shine of her hair and the color of her eyes, to her boots which wouldn't hold up to any job out on Bastien's ranch. The material of her dress was so fine even an eye untrained as his noticed. What made Wyoming unsuited was likely its lack of boutiques and shops selling ribbons and such.

"Is Aster Ridge so different than Chicago?" What was so different that she would visit here and not Kirwin.

"Oh, very. Out here it's windy and dirty. Bastien's home is rather bare. I wonder why he doesn't pick up more furniture for the place. Heaven knows it's large enough." Her face took on a dreamlike quality. "But, you know. It's quite peaceful. I don't sleep well in Chicago, but last night was ... perfect." She waved her hand. "It was probably the exhaustion from traveling. Nothing more."

"I imagine it's a sight quieter out here than in the city."

"It is that. I thought I might sleep until noon with nothing to wake me."

Thomas had to push away the thought of her in bed with her dark copper locks sprawled across her pillow. "Well, I would think Della is right pleased to have you here. She spends her days cooking and cleaning for us men. Being here makes me feel like I must be missin' somethin'."

"What do you mean?"

Thomas shifted in his seat. He hadn't meant to say so much, hadn't even said it out loud to himself. "Oh, just the way they are with one another. Newly wedded, I guess."

Ivete gave a sigh that caused Thomas's heart to rise to his throat. "I know what you mean. My parents were never like that with each other. Maybe you're right. It's because they're so newly in love."

Thomas and Ivete stared at Bastien, his head close to his mother's as they spoke. Until now, he hadn't realized the assumption he'd made. Seeing Bastien and Della, one would expect they'd learned such love from the generation that raised them. To think it was spontaneous made their affection that much more impressive, and to someone like Ivete, it would be quite romantic.

He turned to study Ivete as she watched her family. What type of wife would she be? The suppressed memory of their shared kiss on the side of the tracks rushed over him. The way she'd tilted her mouth up to meet his. Shocked at first, then surrendering. His chest tightened. He must think of anything else - the pain after a long ride, how his shoulders ached at the day's end. When his chest relaxed, he exhaled, thankful.

"So, no wife, Mr. McMullin?"

His temperature rose at the way her eyes danced as she waited for his reply.

"No wife. Can't seem to find one who wants to marry me."

"I don't see the problem. If Bastien hired you, you must have *some* redeeming qualities."

Thomas's lips curved in a smile. "Obviously, if you have to rely on Bastien's opinion of me, conversation isn't one of my greater talents." He drew a deep breath. "I've been working to make my way out here. I was just about to set up a ranch of my own when your brother contacted me, practically begged me to help him." Thomas called the last part over his shoulder so Bastien would hear.

"Whoa, go easy on a guy," Bastien begged. "I asked around, further than Aster Ridge, and the advice was unanimous."

Thomas laughed.

Bastien continued. "Mother, did you know your daughter can't actually saddle a horse? Father has spoiled your last child."

Maxine pursed her lips. "You could do for a lesson in spoiling. Your wife does the work of three maids."

And with that, the conversation turned to preparations for the Grahams' newest addition.

Thomas listened to plans, but his mind was anywhere else. Mostly on the woman who sat next to him. Also on his revelation regarding his desire to be living like Bastien and Della. Was it a wife he wanted? Or a thriving ranch? A baby on the way? Maybe all of those things, but mostly he wanted a love like Bastien had. Like Thomas's parents had shared. With such a partner, one could more easily shoulder the burden of hard work, failed crops, dying cows. Without a companion, life was the same, but lonely.

He glanced at Ivete, she too listened to Maxine and Bastien plan for the baby, yet she didn't join in the planning. Was it possible she too felt a sort of loneliness? One not derived from being without her family, but of pushing against her family's wishes. He'd heard her in the stable, speaking of her broken engagement, of not wanting Bastien to pressure her as her mother did. Was it possible to feel alone when surrounded by a loving family?

THE NEXT MORNING Thomas and the Morris boy, Otto, were mixing feed in the stable. Last night, he'd dreamed of Ivete. Only when he woke, the details slipped from his memory like feed through his hands. The more he moved, the more fell into the bucket below. If he could, he would stand perfectly still and try to gather the dream back to him. As he worked, his mind kept attempting to catch that dream again, to remember her presence. When she arrived in the stable, it was almost a relief to drink in the real her.

She squared her shoulders and lifted her chin. "I decided I would like you to show me how to saddle a horse.

Bastien will not let the issue alone, and I won't give him the satisfaction of teaching me."

Thomas smiled. "Sure." He nodded to Otto and followed Ivete. "Would you like to ride Dusty again?"

"Yes. Which stall is hers?"

Thomas led the way, Ivete falling into step behind him. His back burned. Did she watch him as they walked, or did the heat flaming through him come from his heart wishing she were? He mentally slammed the door on those thoughts. Of course, she wasn't watching him. She had plenty of prospects in her big city. He was too poor for her blood, and she too rich for his.

They stopped at Dusty's stall, and Ivete snaked her way around him. She smelled of lilacs, and he was certain he would suffer from this extra layer of her now in his memory.

Ivete stretched a tender hand toward the horse. "Hello, girl." She spoke softly and pulled an apple from her pocket. The horse sniffed it, gave an approving snort of greeting that fluttered Ivete's skirts, and nibbled the proffered gift.

Thomas stepped inside the stall and leaned against the wall. "How much do you already know?"

Ivete stepped away from the horse. "I know how to saddle a horse, just not so it's fit for riding."

Thomas chuckled.

Ivete smirked then turned to the saddle. "Stand back and let me know when I'm doing something wrong."

As she worked and Thomas offered advice, a sheen of sweat cropped up on her forehead, and she brushed hair from her face with a huff.

Thomas inspected her work over her shoulder. "You're going to need— "

Ivete cut him a look that told him she wasn't ready for any input, thank you kindly.

He bit his lips to prevent the smile that threatened to mock her struggle.

She returned to her task with jerky movements. "I know"—she yanked on the girth—"I just can't ever—" She yanked again, pinching the tender skin on Dusty's belly. The mare stomped her hooves, and Ivete jumped back, reaching for Thomas.

He stepped inside the stall and reached one arm toward her, guiding her behind him. With the other hand, he gripped the harness and calmed the horse. He kept his gaze on Dusty's hindquarters to make sure she didn't try to walk her back legs over and injure Ivete. When the horse was calm, he turned to Ivete who was pressed against the wall of the stall, as far from the horse and saddle as she could get within the tight space. "She can feel your stress."

Ivete pursed her lips and crossed her arms over her chest.

Thomas waved Ivete closer. "She'll forgive you."

Ivete's haughtiness died away when she put a hand on Dusty's head. She leaned her forehead down on the bridge of the horse's long nose. "I'm sorry, girl. I'll be more careful, I promise."

Thomas showed Ivete how to be sure the girth wouldn't pinch and walked around the horse, adjusting small parts of the gear as he went.

He straightened and placed one hand on the saddle. "Do you want the mounting block?"

"Yes." Her voice was sure. "All of this is to make sure I can handle it in a pinch. If I ever needed to mount without it, I'm sure I could. But I'm not going to scramble my way up that horse in front of you or anyone if I can help it."

Thomas hid his grin at the image she'd created and collected the mounting block. When he returned, she was again whispering to Dusty. She led the horse out of her stall and into the aisle of the stable. The lumber was new and filled the air with the scent of freshly cut pine. "Are you and my brother going to fill *all* these stalls?"

"If we don't lose any more to Harder and his gang." They stopped at the mounting block. Anger, old and well-worn, at his wayward friend surged into his chest. He swallowed hard, pushing it down.

"Well, I won't keep you any longer." Ivete hoisted herself into the side-saddle and adjusted her skirts.

Thomas handed her the reins. She plucked them with a gloved hand and met his gaze, holding it until heat flooded his cheeks and he broke the connection.

With a click of her tongue, Ivete kicked her horse into movement. She glanced over her shoulder at him. "Thank you." Then she urged Dusty into a trot.

Thomas looked around the stable. Maybe he could muck a stall. That might be the only activity that could wipe the smell of her from his mind.

8

———

Saddling Dusty that first morning had been more frustration than Ivete had felt in a while, but with two weeks of habitual morning practice, she'd become quite adept. And quite in love with her morning rides to the lake and back. They left her feeling refreshed, like a new woman. And she wasn't the only one learning new things. One morning she returned to the house to find her mother in the kitchen, her hands covered in flour.

"Mother?" Ivete resisted the urge to press her hand to her mother's forehead in case of a fever.

"Ivete, I'm glad you're back. I was helping Della with this bread."

Ivete's eyes fell on the two balls of dough resting on the counter. Mother's was shaggy and powdery, and Della's smooth and round. Similarly, Della's hands were impossibly clean compared to Maxine's, which looked like they might not pull apart if touched together.

"Why don't you come take over? I should take some exercise as well." Her mother stepped around her, ignoring

Ivete's raised eyebrow, and cleaned her hands before exiting the kitchen.

Ivete glanced at Della, and the two burst into giggles.

Della rolled her shoulders and used the back of her hand to wipe her cheek. "You don't need to help. I can manage perfectly on my own. I think your mother was just feeling guilty. I wish I could spend more time with you two, but I can't ride anyways, and I'll be taking time off soon enough." Her eyes moved to her belly and back to Ivete with a knowing smile.

"You're right." Ivete rolled her sleeves, but the blouse wasn't meant for rolling and she couldn't get it past her wrists. She went for her mother's sad ball, but Della put a hand in front of her.

"Why don't you work mine a bit more? I think your mother's roll needs a little help." Della's eyes fairly twinkled.

Ivete laughed. They took their places at the counter and worked the dough. With a few glances at Della, Ivete could tell the technique was to throw all her weight into the dough.

Della spoke without interrupting the flow of her movements. "I have several dresses you could borrow. I hate to watch you wreck your fine city gowns."

Ivete glanced at her hem, days of mud stained the bottom. "I would love that. I thought I'd brought proper attire, but it is wilder out here than I imagined."

Della nodded, leaning into the ball she was working. "Bastien said you're having second thoughts about your wedding." Della lifted her dough and threw it onto the counter with a loud smack. She kept her eyes on the task, allowing Ivete to consider her words without scrutiny.

Ivete followed suit and slammed her ball of dough on the counter. The action was surprisingly satisfying, and she did it again before answering. "I guess I am. I haven't written to him since we arrived. What would I even say?"

Della lifted a shoulder. "That you arrived safely and in time for the birth. That your brother's valley is more beautiful than a dream." She looked sidelong at Ivete, a smirk on her lips.

"It truly is the most beautiful place I've been. That lake ... how did he find this place?"

Della continued to knead, her ball of dough already looking to have recovered from Maxine's efforts. "The plan was to set up closer to the mine, but we had a bit of a problem in Wyoming that forced him to withdraw his inheritance. We ended up not needing it, thank goodness. But I guess once he had all that money, he realized how many options opened up. He didn't have to stick with mining. Instead of working the mine here in Montana, he looked for a place to set up a ranch and hired Thomas."

"Didn't like mining after all?" Ivete gave a small snort. "I knew he was pretending. All those visits home, he would go on and on about how great it was in Wyoming. I can't imagine who would rather be down a mineshaft than in an office near the fire. So what was the problem that forced old bull-headed Bastien to withdraw his inheritance? Last I heard, he was washing his hands of our family's wealth and prosperity."

Della flushed. "It all came out all right in the end." She smiled at the kitchen around her. "Better than all right since the money went to set us up here."

Ivete stopped kneading her dough and shook her hands. Her arms were cramping, and she hadn't even done half as much work as Della.

"It's the counter height." Della dipped her chin at the wooden surface. "Whoever built this home must have been building it for a man, or had a rather tall wife. I would have liked it a bit lower, and *you'd* need a stool to ever be comfortable."

Ivete's short height was a joke in the family. She was a complete anomaly. Every other Graham boasted height, even her mother.

"Let's find me a stool then. Mama says we're here to help. I better figure out how to do all this before the baby comes." She looked around as though the kitchen would have such an item laying around. "I bet there will be something in the stables. We'll ask Thomas."

"You should ask." Della's voice was low and smooth.

Ivete turned to go, but in a blink, caught Della's tone and spun back.

Her sister-in-law was grinning at her, a devilish look in her eyes.

"What?" Ivete lifted her chin.

Della shrugged and covered the dough with white linen towels. "The bread is done for today. We can find you a stool for the next time. Eloise Morris will be here tomorrow to help." She brushed the flour from her hands. "Maybe then I can be a proper host. Now we get to relax a bit. My body hates me." She sliced thick slabs from a loaf of bread and slathered them in butter and jam. Della moved to the table, setting herself in the chair claimed as her's with its small pillow to support her lower back.

Ivete joined Della, and they ate in silence.

Della laid her half-eaten bread on the table. "I was married before, you know."

Ivete's eyes flashed to her sister-in-law. "I did not."

Della gave a slow nod. "It wasn't good." She stopped and drew her eyebrows together. "No, it was worse than that. From what Bastien has told me about your parent's marriage, theirs isn't bad. Maybe their love isn't what it could be, but look at your mother's life. It is nothing to fear. From what I hear, you're trying to decide what is right for you."

Ivete drew a deep breath and closed her eyes, pinching the bridge of her nose. "Honestly, it's the shame that is forefront in my mind. I thought I loved him, but seeing yours and Bastien's affection for one another...." She thought of the way Bastien was drawn to Della as constant as the sun nearing the horizon in the evening. She sucked in a breath and opened her eyes once more. "I see now that the love I had for Henry was more of a love for the life he would provide. A love like my parents have. I might have been able to live with that type of marriage had I not learned about his dalliances. Did Bastien tell you my intended's *woman* approached me?" Ivete shook her head. "My friends were with me. It was humiliating. I was the talk of the town and not because people pitied me. They thought it was my fault, thought my reaction was infantile. Part of me wondered if he hadn't been such a fool, if he had been more discreet, maybe I could have already forgiven him." Ivete heaved a sigh. "If I marry him now, I am accepting his behavior. If I don't marry him, I'm the fool who let Henry Burnham slip away. Other girls won't care that he consorts with such women. Most would be happy with his money and never expect fidelity or love." She barked a bitter laugh. "I guess I am a fool."

"We're all fools. We create these ideas in the solitude of our minds without anyone else to counter them. Then we expect they're true." Della placed a hand on Ivete's arm. "You're the only one who can decide this. You've probably already decided. You just need to find the courage to follow through."

Ivete's throat was thick as she placed her hand on Della's. "I always wanted a sister."

Della's warm smile revealed a deep crease in her cheek that Ivete had never noticed. "Now you have two."

Ivete thought of Angelica and Luc. Their marriage was different from Bastien's, closer to what Ivete's parents shared. "You know, Bastien was right in choosing you over Angelica. He was never the type to let emotion rule. Pragmatic and level-headed, unafraid of the opinion of others." She sighed. "That's always been him. No doubt he knew Angelica could never live this life with him."

"One day, I'll tell you everything. Your brother has plenty of emotion." The corner of Della's mouth lifted at some unknown memory. Ivete finished her lunch, licking the jam off each finger.

She hadn't even stood before Della was on her feet and back in the kitchen and starting the next task. Ivete had been shocked when Bastien arrived in Chicago with a beautiful wife on his arm. She'd been disappointed to have missed the chance to hand-pick a wife from her friends. Once the young women in Chicago had learned Angelica had released Bastien from his commitment, even Angelica's cousin was vying for a chance with him.

Watching her now, Ivete realized just how right Bastien had been to choose her. They had love, but there was more. Their home held a warmth that Ivete had never experienced. It emanated from them, she was certain. Like Thomas had said on that first night, their relationship was something to behold. Now that she'd witnessed it, she wasn't sure how she could ever go back to the cold halls of Chicago. To enter into a loveless marriage for the sake of riches and status.

Before she'd left Chicago, she'd told Henry she wanted

space. Where better to do that than the wide open plains of Montana? Yet, going back now would be like reading the same story twice. The words would be the same, yet they would hold none of the excitement or suspense.

"EVIE, WAKE UP." Bastien's voice pulled her from her dreams.

Ivete gasped, and her eyes flew open to find her brother's face inches from hers. "Hush! Della doesn't want Mother awake yet."

"The baby?" Ivete wiped a hand across her face, trying to clear away her groggy state. She scanned the room, her eyes roving over the unfamiliar space and landing on her dress robe.

"I need you to go tell Thomas to fetch the midwife."

"Of course." She slipped into her robe and pulled on her stockings and boots. When she stood again, Bastien had already disappeared, back to his wife most likely. Ivete's stomach clenched. What reason did her brother have for the concern etched into his features?

An unfamiliar fear spread through her gut as she made her way down the hall and through the back door. The guest house where Thomas slept was not far, but childhood books about wolves and bears crept into her mind as she stood on the threshold. Her eyes flashed across the vast prairie that surrounded Bastien's ranch. The space was blue with moonlight, but shadows clung to every corner. When no shapes appeared, she bolted for the thatched roof of the guest house. When she reached it, she pounded on the door with the side of her fist. She threw furtive glances over her shoulder. Was that shadow a bear? Was that a wolf howling she heard in the distance? Was it getting closer? She pounded faster. Did coyotes—no! She wouldn't drive herself into a hysterical terror through her imagination alone. There were real things to be scared of tonight— she remembered the fear in Bastien's eyes. She shut a door on her imaginings, blocked out the shape-shifting shadows, and focused on the man behind the locked door. "Thomas!"

When Thomas didn't open the door immediately, she tried the latch and stumbled inside the darkened house. She closed the door and leaned against it, sucking lungfuls of air. The moonlight cast a soft glow through the windows and lit the spacious room.

"Thomas?" she called into the open space. Having never been inside the guest house, she hadn't a clue which way to begin searching for him. She pushed away from the door and opened her mouth to call again when Thomas appeared around a corner to her right, the light from outside illuminating his bare chest.

Ivete let out a gasp not only of surprise but at the impropriety of being in a room with a half-naked man. Quick as a whip, she raised a hand to cover her eyes. "Bastien wants you to go for the midwife." She peeked through her fingers.

Thomas pulled a shirt over his head, the billowing fabric falling to the top of his legs in less than an instant.

She let out a sigh of relief. If this were Chicago, this mere encounter would have ruined any chance she had to wed a man like Henry Burnham.

Thomas hopped on one bare foot, shoving the other into a boot. "Already? Why are *you* here? Is Della ..."

"I don't know a thing. I just came to fetch you." Ivete turned back to the house. The yellow glow of lantern light shone from Bastien and Della's shared bedroom. Yet another difference between theirs and her parent's relationship.

"Let's go check." Thomas brushed his hand down Ivete's upper arm, as he walked past and gestured her through the door, his eyes black in the darkness.

They rushed through the grass to the main house. Somehow, though Thomas held no weapons, Ivete's earlier fears of prowling creatures had dissipated entirely. Her only thought was for her sister-in-law and the worry her brother faced.

Thomas opened the door and allowed Ivete to enter first. His breath was hot in her hair as she led the way to Bastien's bedroom. Murmuring came from inside, and Ivete rapped softly on the wooden door.

Bastien appeared, yanking the door open with such force Ivete crashed backward into Thomas's chest.

"Thank the Lord." Her brother sighed. "Can you go for the midwife?"

"May I?" Thomas asked, lifting a finger to point into the bedroom.

Ivete shot him an incredulous look. What a bold query! To ask to enter a married woman's chamber!

He stepped forward without an invitation.

Her jaw almost hit the floor.

Thomas addressed Della directly. "When did the pains start?"

Bastien released the door and joined Thomas at the bedside. "Maybe an hour."

"Longer," Della groaned from her bed. "Two or—" Her gritting teeth cut off her words as her face tightened in pain.

Bastien knelt on the floor near the bed, his hands hovering over his wife's suffering.

Thomas stepped nearer, eyeing Della. "Has there been any fluid?"

Both Bastien and Ivete whipped their heads to gawk at Thomas.

Della let out a deep breath. "Not yet." The pain seemingly disappeared. With Bastien's help, she heaved from the bed and paced the length of their bed.

"I'll go now." He turned and breezed past Ivete and through the door, leaving his familiar scent of peppermint behind.

Ivete couldn't tear her eyes from Bastien and Della. Her sister-in-law stopped her bedside vigil and braced her forearms against the wall. Bastien rubbed circles on her back. Ivete felt like an interloper. They didn't even notice her. She wanted to leave, but she stood transfixed by her brother's worried devotion. His relationship with his wife was like nothing she'd ever seen.

When the door opened again, Ivete jumped and spun, eyes wide.

"Ivete." Thomas jerked his head toward the hallway.

Relief flooded her stomach as she followed Thomas out of the bedroom.

"Thank you. I didn't know— "

"They need hot water and dry towels. Start the water immediately." He twisted one way, then another. "Bastien has paper to line the bed, but you'll have to ask him where it is." He stopped and must have noticed Ivete's lack of movement. He stepped nearer and gripped Ivete by her shoulders, squinting at her face. "Are you okay?"

At his question, Ivete's knees threatened to collapse. She locked them and nodded. Her eyebrows clashed in determination. "Yes. I'll start the water right away."

Thomas nodded and released her, pivoting to open the stove. He threw another log inside and closed the door. "It will be a while yet. Keep that stove fed. I'll be back before you know it."

He turned to go, and Ivete reached for his back, wishing she could adopt his cool demeanor. The door closed with an echoing thud, reminding her that she was on her own.

She swallowed her fears and set to work, searching for the largest pot in Della's kitchen. In the back of a corner cupboard, she found one larger than her torso. With a heave, she carried it outside to the water pump. As she worked the handle, she glanced around for the wild animals that might think her a tasty snack. Her hands ached on the cool metal of the pump. When the pot was almost half-way filled, her groggy mind realized that she would never be able to carry it inside.

She stood with one hand on the cast metal and contemplated whether to dump what she'd pumped and use small pots to fill the rest or to disturb Bastien. Her aching hands decided for her. She strode into the house and knocked on Bastien's bedroom door.

When her brother opened the door, his hair was standing at attention as if he'd run his hands through it multiple times. Behind him, Della paced the room. She stopped, gripped the bedpost, and scrunched her face. When the pain was over, Bastien nodded at Ivete's request for assistance with the water and placed her in his spot next to Della before leaving. This close, Ivete saw Della had a sheen of sweat on her face. She pressed her fist into her back and Ivete remembered how Bastien had rubbed it for her. Would such ministrations from Ivete be welcomed? Since Ivete's arrival, Della had done nothing but hard labor, and yet, this was a labor of an entirely different sort.

Ivete wrung her hands. "Thomas has gone for the

midwife. I am boiling water, and"—Ivete scanned the bedroom—"Thomas mentioned paper for something?"

"Yes, the bed. Bastien and I already laid them out." Della panted.

"Oh, wonderful." Ivete curled her fingers into her dressing gown, wishing she could comfort Della in some way. "Are you very scared?" Hopefully, the answer would be 'no.'

The edges of Della's face shone with sweat, but she smiled. "God made women to do this. I'm no more worried about delivering this baby than I am about riding a horse."

Ivete shook her head, smiling slowly. "You are a wonder."

"She certainly is. She's also afraid of horses." Bastien entered the room, smiling at his wife with such love that Ivete gulped and took a step back.

Bastien jerked his head toward the kitchen. "I think that is enough water for now. If we fill it much more, it won't be warm until Christmas."

Ivete smiled, grateful for not having to pump any more water and for her brother's comforting countenance. "When will you wake Mother?"

"That is up to my dear wife."

Della glared at Bastien. "That was supposed to stay between you and me, dear husband. I don't want anyone up before they need to be." She softened her gaze. "Now poor Ivete is awake with nothing to do. *You* should have fetched Thomas and filled the pot."

"Yes, you are right as always, my dear." He leaned forward and kissed Della's forehead. "Evie." He turned to her. "You may go to sleep. Thank you for your help."

Ivete widened her eyes. "You think I can go to sleep *now*?

I've never felt so awake. I think I could swim across your pond."

Nevertheless, she left the room, leaving them to each other. She walked down the darkened hallway and into the kitchen. The moon shone in as it had in Thomas's little house. She coaxed the coals in the fireplace into a small flame and placed a short piece of wood on top, settling into an armchair close by. Images of Thomas filled her mind. First, his bare chest, then his determined face as he'd commanded Bastien's bedroom. His apparent knowledge when it came to birth. Now he was out there, seeking the midwife amidst all those creatures Ivete feared.

She tried to picture Henry being so gallant and brave. The more she compared the two, the more she found herself admiring Thomas's strengths over Henry's. But if she put the man aside, and imagined her future, Henry won hands down. A woman would have to be mad to choose a life of toil, like Della's, over a life of comfort and security. And yet, since her arrival, Ivete hadn't once found herself wishing to be back in Chicago. She chewed her lip in thought. She hadn't even picked up a book. Either she'd been too busy, or possibly living the life portrayed in those books, was turning out to be more enjoyable than reading about it. Now that Della was having a baby, who would be there to assume Della's responsibilities? Ivete straightened her back. She'd watched Della work over the last several days. Surely Ivete could handle a few of the more important tasks until that neighbor girl came to help.

9

Thomas's horse followed the midwife's mount to the Grahams' valley. She and her mount rode all over this area and had delivered almost every person in their part of Montana under the age of twenty. She knew this country better than Thomas, better than most folk who had lived here since their birth. Like a sparrow knows the lay of the land better than the four-legged creatures that stay to their paths through the brush and trees.

Thomas cleared his throat. "How many babies have you delivered, Claudia?"

"One hundred and two. One hundred and three after today. A mite more than you have, I believe."

As the pair crested the last of the rolling hills, the Grahams' home came into view, a prick of light in the dark. Thomas's mount quickened its pace, no doubt anxious for his bed and oats. Food and bed called to Thomas, as well. A warm glow shone behind the eastern ridge promising to soon spread its rays over the valley.

Claudia kicked her horse, urging it forward faster. When they arrived, she climbed off her horse, slid her saddlebag over her shoulder, and tossed her reins to Thomas before making her way inside the home. Thomas led both horses to the stables. He lifted the saddle from his horse when the whisper of hay alerted him to someone's arrival.

He looked up to find Ivete, that same lost look on her face as she'd worn in Bastien and Della's bedroom. She was unused to the stress of childbirth, that was clear. But he'd seen that lost look on her face before, when they'd traveled from the train station to Aster Ridge. He could blame it on the shock of nearly being kidnapped by Aaron's gang. And yet... he knew there was more to her than she revealed. Was it possible breaking her engagement had left her unmoored and unable to navigate her life? Out here, her happiness fairly shone out of her. He recalled the teasing smile she gave Bastien as she called his lake a pond. Or how she held her chin when she sat high atop a horse.

He set the saddle on its peg and leaned an elbow on the warm leather. "How is she doing?"

Ivete raised her eyebrows and heaved a sigh. "No baby yet. I never knew it took so long."

He stepped to Claudia's horse and removed the bridle and bit from its mouth. He left the saddle and gave the creature a bowl of oats. Claudia had risen in the night to tend Della. The least they could do was to feed her horse handsomely.

Ivete stroked the horse's mane. "How did you know what to do? You were so calm."

Thomas gave a huff of mirth. "I'm the second of eleven kids. More if you count the ones in heaven. I've been around for a birth or two. Plus, Bastien and I prepared for this. I was always going to be the one who went for the midwife when the time came." A smile played on his lips as he remembered the relief on her face when he'd come into the

Grahams' bedroom the second time. Then, when he had directed her in the kitchen, he'd seen resolve bloom on her face as she went from afraid to determined. A flicker of pride ballooned in his chest, though logic told him he had no reason for any claim on her actions. "You didn't do too bad yourself. Did you get the water boiled?"

Ivete gave a hard laugh, "I filled it up outside and had to get Bastien to haul it inside for me."

Ivete squatted to collect a brush from the bucket then slid her small hand inside the leather strap. She ran the bristles in waves along Thomas's horse. He watched her for a moment before turning away. When she was in this stable, speaking softly to the animals, he easily forgot she was a proper city lady. Put her in plain calico with a braid down her back and she might be any of the women Thomas saw at church. Only none of them lingered in his mind all the day.

He moved through the mundane tasks of feeding the rest of the stock. Pulled from sleep by the unusual midnight action, the other horses stirred, and he didn't plan on going back to bed any time soon. Ivete stayed busy with small tasks like sweeping hay from the aisle or brushing a horse's mane. Thomas watched her from the corner of his eyes, wondering if she stayed because she welcomed his presence, or if she was loath to go back inside for some other reason. If Thomas's life had prepared him for the drama involving a birth, Ivete's had done the opposite. She was older in age, but young in knowledge of the world. Finally, neither could think of anything else to do and they made their way back to the house.

Maxine and Bastien were in the main room. Bastien paced, his hair still sticking up at all angles.

"Did the midwife say how close?" Thomas asked.

Bastien stopped pacing and met Thomas's gaze. He shook his head and continued wearing a path in the rug.

The Grahams kept a small spirits cabinet near the fireplace. Thomas went and poured a large glass of brandy for his friend and pushed it into Bastien's hands. "Della is strong. Have you seen that woman knead dough? She's going to do wonderfully. Claudia is here. Do you know what she told me on the way here, Bastien? She'd helped deliver over a hundred healthy babes. Yours will soon be added to that number. Della is in good hands."

Thomas offered drinks to the women, but only Maxine accepted one. Ivete was beginning to get a wild look similar to Bastien's. Her eyes were wide and her hair had come undone from its braid, curling around her face like a wild halo. He glanced around the home, trying to think of something for her to do.

His gaze landed on the empty kitchen, a space that was rarely, if ever, vacant. "Ivete, will you help me? I'm sure Della will be famished once the work of birthing is done. Let's throw together some pancakes."

She followed him into the kitchen like a wraith. The steam from the boiling water filled the air and coated the windows. Thomas opened every drawer in his search for the necessary utensils. Della had a small crock of buttermilk, and he passed it to Ivete. "Pour all that in." Ivete did as she was told, and the cream coated the bottom of the bowl. He set a sack of ground flour on the counter. "Four cups of this."

They worked together, Thomas passing her eggs and her cracking them, then stirring until they had a lumpy batter. Thomas dipped his finger to taste it and turned to collect the salt bowl. He slid the large pot to the back of the stove and retrieved a skillet from where it hung on the wall.

"Once that heats, we'll be set." He looked at Bastien,

wondering if it would be inappropriate to give the man a task, maybe ask him to collect eggs from the coop. The alcohol was gone from Bastien's cup, but his eyes still raged with that inner storm. Thomas bit the inside of his cheek. Best not to make any requests after all. The man's wife struggled in the next room. He might break the eggs with his shaking hands.

As though to prove Thomas's thoughts, Della cried out. Bastien shot up and thundered down the hall. Maxine and Ivete looked at one another as silence hung in the air. A log in the stove broke, interrupting the quiet, but all remained frozen. Another of Della's cries came, this time followed by the familiar mew of a newborn baby.

Maxine let out a breath and fell into the seat behind her. Ivete's eyes brightened and she turned from the forgotten bowl of batter to Thomas. He reached for her and she flung her arms around his neck. Laughing, Thomas swung her in a circle before releasing her with a grin. Her hand traveled from his shoulder down his arm and she gripped his hands with both of hers.

The moment was fleeting as she released her grip to rush down the hall. The distinct creak of their bedroom door told him she'd finally found the strength to be in the room with all its stresses.

Thomas went to Maxine. Kneeling at her feet, he placed a hand on her knee. "You have your first grandchild."

Maxine's eyes misted as she pressed her lips together to stave off the tears. He stood and offered his hand. "Shall you go take a look?" She nodded and laid her fingers in his palm. He ushered her through the bedroom and closed the door on the family before retreating down the hall. A pang of longing reverberated through his chest as he thought of his mother. Gone now, dead after the birth of Thomas's sister, Anna.

He glanced at the spirits cabinet. Bastien would not begrudge him a drink on such a day. But his father's old advice rang in his ears. "When you drink to forget, the only thing you lose is who you are." The day Thomas and Aaron had learned of Missy Jones's betrayal and subsequent refusal of either boy, they'd bought a few jars of moonshine from a local distiller. Thomas had woken in the morning in the barn with a raging headache. Add to it, that the hay he'd slept in had been filled with hungry fleas and Thomas had learned a lesson without the need for words. But his father wasn't one to let an opportunity pass. After his father had passed on his words about drinking, he'd continued. " If you don't mind losing yourself to the bottle, you go right on drinkin' and stick to the barn for your bed."

Funny, how that childhood lesson captained his actions this day. Instead of pouring himself a drink, he returned to the task of making pancakes. The pan was plenty hot, and he poured and flipped until all the batter was used. He took a few for himself, then left a stack on the counter as he made his way out the door.

CLOSE TO MID-DAY, Bastien found him, a smile on his face as he clapped Thomas on the back.

"Thank you. You were more helpful than I ever knew you could be."

Thomas chuckled at the half-hearted compliment. "Congratulations. Boy or girl?"

"Girl." Bastien's face was dreamlike. "She has her mother's dark hair. Her eyes are blue, but my mother says they all start that way."

Thomas shook his head. "You know, a daughter means you'll be fending off suitors in about sixteen years."

Bastien laughed through his nose. "Sooner, if she grows up to look like her mother. A word of warning: don't marry a beautiful woman. Settle for plain." A smile played on his lips, "She did a fine job. This morning I would have done anything to prevent another birth. Now, I can't help but want a slew of them."

Thomas chuckled. "Don't tell Della that. Even a woman as kind as her would probably find something to throw at your head."

Talk turned from pregnant wives to pregnant mares. Bastien's knowledge grew so quickly Thomas wouldn't be needed beyond his year commitment. And once Thomas fulfilled his contract, he could start his own ranch, a haven for his siblings. His goal for so many years, and yet the prospect of leaving Aster Ridge made the corners of his mouth fall.

10

Ivete readied for her daily ride with a flutter in her stomach. She'd worked with Della to put a hem in a skirt so she had a sturdier and more casual dress for riding. Ivete's habit was too muddy to be worn, and she didn't dare ask Della to help wash it. She buttoned herself into the vest, her face warming as she recalled her dream the night before. In it Thomas was bare chested as he had been when she'd gone into the guest house. The knowledge that he slept shirtless had worked itself into her brain, and she couldn't chase the image out of her head. It floated in her periphery all day and, apparently, all night.

She entered the stables with her heart in her throat, but Thomas wasn't in sight and didn't find her as he usually did. By now, she was capable of saddling her horse. She'd known most of everything before she came, and daily rides had perfected the skill. She still hesitated every time she tightened the girth. Afraid one day, she'd nip the horse's belly, and it would tread on her toes. But she used Thomas's trick of putting her hand in the spot under the seam, getting much closer to the animal's feet than she wanted but preventing the unwanted pinch.

Once she saddled her horse, Ivete considered finding Thomas to check her work and make sure Dusty was safe to ride but shook off the idea. She was never going to get the image of him out of her head if she sought him out at every chance. She glanced toward the entrance to the stable. The sun shone bright. She twisted her mouth. If she had a hat, she'd not have to squint, but the one and only hat she'd brought with her was long gone, crushed on her first day here. Not that the flimsy thing would do her much good right now. What she needed was something stout like what Bastien and Thomas wore. She strode into the stables. Surely there would be something useful lying around. She entered the office with wandering eyes. Ah. There, hung high on the wall, a wide-brimmed hat crying for a head. She'd never seen Bastien wear it. Maybe it was a spare. Likely he'd never miss it. She lifted it from its home and planted it on her head. The band was too big, but with her hair in a knot the fit was quite comfortable. The wide brim would serve to keep her face and neck from freckling in the sun.

She led the mare to the mounting block and climbed on, adjusting her skirts. Without a partner, she stayed within sight of the stable, not venturing to the lake.

Last night's dream settled in her mind once again. It had been both fantasy and nightmare. First Thomas had been blessedly topless, but soon Henry's lover came into the picture and spat at Ivete like she'd done on the street in Chicago. The awful woman claimed Thomas, putting her hand on his chest, and Ivete was left looking for Henry but unsure she wanted to find him. Ridiculous. No woman would choose Thomas when she had Henry Burnham in her palm. But that piece of logic didn't prevent Ivete's neck from flushing with jealousy.

As she rode along the fenceline that circled Bastien and Della's home, Ivete tried to imagine herself holding Thomas with the same ownership as Henry's woman had. No matter how she tried, Ivete's touch was tentative, not experienced like the woman's. No wonder Henry used her services. Ivete didn't have the experience to please a man. Her stomach lurched at the thought of trying. It settled itself once again with the image of Thomas, a vision she found both safe and comfortable. She wouldn't mind fumbling her way into learning to please a man like him. She bit her lip. No woman of class would dare venture into the territory her mind seemed determined to stray this morning. She scoffed. Why shouldn't she? No. Ridiculous thought. Impossible. Women did not ... they could not ... Henry's mistress's face swam before her vision. Perhaps women could, but it certainly was not done in Ivete's social class. Even her reaction to finding out about Henry's indiscretions had been scandalous fodder for polite Chicago society. Women didn't speak of these things, they didn't shout at their fiance's and they definitely endured the gossip until it passed instead of running away to spend their days in obscurity.

But ... she wasn't currently in polite Chicago society. She wasn't in Chicago at all. In fact, she was so far away from Chicago, it was likely no one would ever find out.

No one would ever know if she took a lover. If Henry could have dalliances, why shouldn't she? She wouldn't be the first woman to learn a few things before her wedding. The thought of marrying Henry further enraged her. It seemed no matter what she did, Henry would always have the upper hand. He would be the one doing whatever he pleased while she sat prim at home like her mother. She shook her head. Mother was content with her role, happy even, but Ivete was of a different generation and she was stubbornly determined to balance the scales. No matter that the idea of doing such unknown things with a man made her stomach clench and her lungs desperate for air. She wouldn't enter into an unequal marriage. If she wanted to please her family and wed Henry, she was left with one choice.

With her mind made up and her heart in her throat, Ivete turned her horse for home and urged Dusty into a canter. Thomas stood in the yard when she arrived, looking strong and golden in the bright sun. If she was going to do this, she had to be bold. Forget the mounting block. Ivete steered her horse toward Thomas. Her hair had fallen with the gallop and the over-large hat's movement on her head. She brushed the stray hairs behind her shoulders. "Good morning, Thomas." She hoped her voice had the purr she'd imagined on her ride.

"Look at you, Ms. Graham. Saddled up without any help from me."

"I looked, but you were nowhere in sight." Ivete turned her lips into a pout and watched him under the rim of her hat. "Will you help me down?"

Thomas stepped forward to grip her waist and lowered her from the mare.

"You make it look easy." Ivete didn't step away. Instead she forced herself to hold her position a few inches from his frame. She raked his gaze from his eyes to his lips.

Something like fear crossed his face, and he took a step back. He nodded and eyed her hat. "You found a hat."

Ivete narrowed her eyes, wondering if he recognized the item from the office. She didn't acknowledge his comment. She stepped closer, instead, closing the gap to pluck at the buttons on his shirt. She had little experience of her own with men, of course. With three older brothers, no man dared teach her anything in the ways of seduction. But her friends had discussed their dalliances with suitors or cousins. She was not completely without knowledge. She raised her chin and closed her eyes, not bold enough to pucker her lips.

Thomas cleared his throat, and her eyes flew open. She twisted her lips to the side and lowered her brows at him.

"Are you feeling well?" He looked pointedly at her hand on his waist, which she promptly dropped and hid in her borrowed cotton skirt.

"Perfect." The more she looked at him, the more she wanted him. Was this all it took? Was making a decision like this the same as turning the dial on a lantern? But she knew if she turned it too high it would burn and blacken the glass rim. She hesitated, waiting for him to do his part, whatever that was.

He gave her a quizzical look before turning and walking back into the darkness of the stable. She watched him move away, wishing she had a reason to keep him close. For the first time, she possessed an inkling of understanding for Henry's actions. Possibly he met his woman at the archery club. They had a shared interest, and emotions ensued. While the other woman hadn't been beautiful, not like women in Ivete's class were, a kindred spirit can go a long way when it comes to attraction. She heaved a sigh when Thomas closed the office door behind him.

She knocked the hat onto her back, the leather strap tightening on her throat and keeping it from falling to the ground. She led Dusty to her stall and went through the routine of unsaddling and brushing down the animal. Now that Ivete had made up her mind, her heart raced at how to communicate her desire to Thomas. A nervous giggle bubbled from her lips as she tried to picture herself being so forward with any man.

Once Dusty was tended, Ivete could wait no longer. She made her way to the office and leaned on the frame. "Thomas."

His gaze moved from the papers on the desk to her face. When she didn't say anything, he knit his brows. "Yes?"

Now that the moment had come, her courage faltered, and she swallowed, her throat dry as the desert. "Thank you. I used your trick to get the saddle on properly."

As always, talk of horses soothed him. His brows smoothed, and he leaned back in his chair, lifting his hands to cradle the back of his head. "I'm glad I could help." He lifted a brow. "I know Bastien was giving you grief about doing it yourself, and I'm glad you've perfected it, but you know I'm happy to help any time"

"Yes." She eyed his position behind the desk, trying to determine the best way to approach him. She huffed and glanced at the door. "I wondered ... would you like to go fishing with me tomorrow? Bastien thinks I should not go alone."

"I'd be happy to accompany you."

Ivete reigned in a smile. "Okay then. I'll be off."

As she made her way to the house, she played the scene over in her mind. She had no clue what more she could have done, but she was determined to find out before they went fishing tomorrow.

BACK AT THE HOUSE, Ivete was startled to see a new girl in the kitchen. She wasn't kneading dough as Della was always doing, but on her knees scrubbing the floors.

Ivete pulled off her gloves. "Hello?"

The girl sat back on her haunches and dipped her head. "Miss."

"Are you the new maid?"

"Yes, ma'am." The girl stood, pushing a blonde curl away from her face. She kept her eyes downcast. "I'm Eloise Morris."

Standing, Ivete could see the girl's figure. She looked young, but had more curves than Ivete and looked well-fed. "Pleased to meet you, Eloise. We are all glad you're here. Is everyone in Della's room?"

"I believe."

With a nod, Ivete made her way to her room to change out of her riding clothes. She could hear talking through the walls and smiled at how well her mother and Della were getting along.

When she joined them, Maxine cradled the baby in her arms, a look of utter adoration on her face.

Ivete smiled. "Grandmotherhood suits you. You're absolutely glowing."

Her eyes lifted to Ivete's. "You were this beautiful too, you know." Her gaze moved to Della. "I bet you were a lovely baby. All that dark hair and eyebrows. Most babies look like bald old men." Her warm smile touched Ivete's heart. Maxine was happy in Chicago, but here she bloomed like one of the wild daisies along the ridge. Her smiles were frequent, and her laugh easy. Bastien had been right when he'd said time in the country was what she needed.

Ivete sat on the bed next to Della. "And how are you doing, new mama?"

"Tired." Della's eyes were heavy.

"Can we take little Violet out so you can rest?"

"Maybe for a bit." She stifled a yawn with the back of her hand. "Claudia said to nurse her every few hours. I think we still have a bit of time."

Ivete nodded and stood. "Come, Mother, let us give Della a rest."

Behind her, her mother cooed and crooned. "You're my little bundle, aren't you. All mine right now. Not even your daddy can have you. I'll give you back to Mommy, but not yet, little one."

Ivete suppressed a laugh. She'd never seen her mother be so saccharine.

A small seating area was nestled up against the side of the house, surrounded by roses, and though the weather cooled day by day, several blooms remained, casting their scent over the seats. Ivete and her mother settled there with Violet.

Ivete slumped into the seat with a happy sigh. "I wish their kitchen wasn't in the middle of the house. Maybe they can put up a wall now that Della has help. She's not going to want to stare at someone else doing the work all day."

"No." Her mother grinned at the baby in her lap. "This house wasn't made for *our* type of people. I suppose whoever built it expected to work as hard as Della does. I hope Bastien keeps this girl on after we go."

"She's a bit pretty, don't you think?" Ivete recalled the girl's youth and slim figure. Her wide eyes and her timid face as she answered Ivete's questions.

Maxine lifted her eyebrows in agreement, "Yes, but *I* didn't hire her. Men usually want their maids young and pretty."

"Oh, stop, Mama." Ivete's cheeks heated, and she

regretted bringing it up. "Not every man is like that. *Bastien* isn't like that."

Her mother pressed her lips together, disbelief evident on her face.

"Did *you* ever have an affair?" Ivete asked, her eyes glued to her mother's face as she awaited a reply.

Her mother's jaw dropped as she placed a hand over Violet's only uncovered ear as though shielding the infant from Ivete's crass question. "Of course I haven't. What do you think of me?" She smacked her lips. "You young girls these days. Next thing, you'll be wearing breeches."

"I didn't mean any offense. I only wondered if it is common among the men, why can't it be common among the women? I mean, you're already married, so there's no virginity to speak of."

Her mother's head shook as though she were an over-heated teakettle. "That Angelica has told you too much."

"Not just Angelica, Mother. Among all the girls back home, I am the least knowledgeable about these things." She kept her eyes on the baby as she spoke. "It's a bit embarrassing."

"Oh, pish. You are doing right in the sight of God."

"Does God not care about what His sons are doing? I see no consequences for them. Worse, from you, I hear only about the expectation of sin."

Her mother straightened, narrowing her eyes at Ivete. "You said your naivete is an embarrassment to you. Quit acting like a witless schoolgirl and accept the ways of the world. It was not created for women. It was built for men. Women and beast alike were put here to serve them. You should be happy that your expectation of serving means turning a blind eye and not"—she lifted her hand and gestured toward the house—"to slave all day."

Ivete stared at the tall pines at the treeline, another of God's creations living as he intended. Strong and free. Tears burned behind her eyes. Her mother rarely spoke to her in such a manner. She was unsure how to respond, afraid anything she could say would bring on a lecture.

Finally, she stood, wishing she'd never come in from her ride. "That is not the God I know. Men manipulated this world to benefit themselves. God did not make it so."

She turned and marched for the barn, intending to find Thomas and somehow recapture that giddiness he unknowingly cultivated.

As she approached the barn, she heard the murmur of voices. Her steps slowed, but she forced herself to round the corner anyway.

Bastien leaned against the doorframe of the office. He turned at her approach, and a smile broke on his face. "Sister, you are flushed. Is this Montana air too hot for your liking?"

"It is just fine." She stopped, and he placed an arm around her shoulders, turning them both to face Thomas, who stood in front of his desk, leaning against it with his ankles crossed. "It is Mother who isn't to my liking."

Bastien laughed, shaking Ivete as his chest heaved. "I've always found her to be quite pleasant."

"Yes, well, that is because you are a man and God's chosen gender. The rest of us are beasts."

Bastien's jovial face fell. With a nod to Thomas, he steered Ivete away from the office down the long aisle of the barn. "You are not a beast of any sort, and I'm sure Mother doesn't think you one."

"You know nothing of what it is like to be a woman."

"You're right." He removed his arm from around her and

opened a stall. A mother and colt lay together, the baby's long legs tangled like a pretzel.

"Oh." Ivete's heart softened. Something strong and inexplicable drew her further into the stall. The mother horse lifted her head to survey Ivete. Deeming her not a threat, she lay her head down again. Or maybe she was simply too exhausted to care about a stranger overmuch.

"When was she born?"

"Last night. All babies come in the night."

They stood together in awed silence for a moment before Bastien broke the reverence. "So, is this argument with Mother about Henry?"

"Everything is about Henry. She is utterly convinced that marriage to him is right. Worse, she doesn't listen or believe when I tell her I don't want to go through with it."

"I imagine now that you've broken off the engagement, he will find himself a new bride, and mother's ideas will not matter."

Ivete swallowed and glanced up at Bastien.

He narrowed his eyes. "You are guilty of something. I recognize that face from when you lost my fishing pole in the lake."

Ivete smiled and hoped he would be as forgiving now. "I haven't broken the engagement. We fought, then I left. Nothing was set or broken."

Bastien's brows knit as he studied her. "Have you written to him?"

Ivete shook her head. "What would I even say? I cannot pretend as Mama does. Yet, I don't know if I'm ready to break it off completely."

The colt raised at her voice and pressed itself onto its hooves. Ivete knelt and let him lip her palm. "He is well-bred, and the coloring is stunning. He will be a fine mount."

"You'll forgive Henry?"

She pinched the bridge of her nose. "I cannot forgive it, but maybe I can live with it."

"Not all men do such things."

"You fled from society. Do you expect me to run away and do the same? Marry someone like Thomas?" The idea, though thrown out as an absurd option, stirred warmth into her belly. With a shake of her head, she threw off the thought. "I cannot slave as Della does."

Bastien laughed again, his usual humor slipping into the seriousness of their conversation. "Has Mother been in your ear about me as well? Do you both think I abuse her so?"

"I don't understand why she must work. You have more than enough funds to allow her a life of luxury." Ivete let out a whisper of a laugh. "I daresay she's wondering why she married you in the first place."

"It wasn't for my money, only my height and my sense of humor. You, my sister, have neither to boast about."

Ivete barked a laugh at his tease.

Bastien put an elbow in her ribs. "Della doesn't need to work, and neither would you. So long as you gain our parent's approval, your dowry will be sufficient."

"Well, Mama seems set on Henry Burnham. She would reject any other man."

"It isn't up to Mother." He lifted a brow. "Father would be the one to give— or not give you— your dowry. Do you still care to curse the rules of gender?"

Ivete shot a glare at Bastien, who tucked his lips between his teeth and rolled his eyes to the ceiling in an expression of innocence.

They left the stall, and as they made their way down the length of the barn, Bastien hooked his arm around Ivete's neck and pulled her close to plant a kiss on the top of her head. "You'll make the right decision for you. Nobody can tell you what you can live with. Just remember your options aren't Henry or Thomas, though I daresay you could do a sight worse than Thomas. There are plenty of other men. Come out here, and you'll see for yourself how hungry these western territories are for women. I'm certain you'd find one as rich as Burnham. Thomas and I are small fish compared to those who have already made it big in the cattle industry."

"Boys playing men, huh?" She pushed away from him and smiled at the easy camaraderie they shared. Her brother was a true testament that good men were to be found if only one searched hard enough. She drew a deep breath. If she'd started looking sooner, before she'd met Henry, everything might be different. Taking time to search now might result in losing Henry altogether. Aversions to commitment and sowing wild oats might be acceptable for men, but such traits from a woman would be absolutely scandalous.

11

With Bastien's baby but two weeks old, the arrival of fall ushered in cold damp mornings that forced Thomas to work quickly to keep blood pulsing through his extremities. After breakfast Thomas saddled his horse, Boomer, to search for a missing cow that hadn't made his way back for mealtime. Dread weighed heavy in Thomas's chest as he rode in search of the lost cattle. Most likely this bull had fallen to the same illness as the other three they'd already lost. Many more, and they wouldn't have any remaining beasts to sell.

When he came upon a cow lying on the ground any lingering hope left him. His shoulders sagged, and he rubbed a palm down his face. The cow's sides rose and fell with its rapid breathing, but it would not even raise its head at Thomas's approach. Boomer pranced, jittery, his feet moving as though he wanted to take them far away from the danger. Thomas pulled his rifle from the scabbard that hung from his saddle. He removed the bandana from his neck and lay it over the animal's rolling eyes. He pressed the lever action forward on his rifle and pulled it back again, chambering the shell.

The shot rang in the chilly, open air. Boomer whinnied and cantered backward, shaking his head. Thomas whistled, and the animal returned to his side, though its feet never stayed in the same place for more than a second. Thomas mounted and urged Boomer for the stables to collect a spade. He and Boomer's day was far from over. He tried to focus on the sweet foal just born, but the shadow of death was too close to shake.

Once Thomas dug the grave and maneuvered the two-thousand-pound animal, he was drenched in sweat. With the cow buried, he could return to the ranch. The sun was high and he hoped to find lunch when he arrived.

As he rode toward the house, he flattened his lips as he considered their season. He and Bastien would have to take the cows to market early. The beasts weren't yet big enough to get the best price, but losing one cow a week was costing them far more in potential income. He thought once more on the lost mares and cursed Aaron Harder's name. Losing cows. Losing mares. Maybe ranching wasn't as steady a life as he'd once thought.

THOMAS FOUND the kitchen a whirl of activity. Bastien was holding little Violet, Maxine next to him and looking at the babe with shining eyes.

Thomas approached and took a seat next to Bastien. "Just buried another cow."

Bastien's smile fell. "How many does that make?"

"Six altogether."

Bastien sighed. "Should we take them to market early?"

Thomas nodded. "That was my thought. We'll get more for them small than we will dead."

Bastien sniffed at Thomas's halfhearted humor, then said, "You'll have to go once Strawberry gives birth. I think there will be enough time before Raven is ready. Worst case, I call Smith, and he can help deliver."

Thomas made a face. "And charge you enough to feed the stable for a week."

Bastien laughed. "Surely his rates aren't that high."

Thomas lifted his brows and gave Bastien a pointed look. He and Bastien had birthed a foal the night before, and Raven might not be due for more than a week. How many cows would they lose, waiting to save money by Thomas assisting in the birth and not hiring Smith?

Maxine's voice cut into his thoughts. "This is all too dreary, and I can positively feel the stress coming off you both. It is a beautiful day and you are young." She turned to the kitchen and hitched her voice higher. "Eloise, darling, fix another sandwich for Thomas and wrap everything up. These kids are going on a picnic."

Before he knew it, Maxine was pressing a basket into his arms and shuffling him and Bastien out the door. She took the baby from Della and promised to send Eloise if Violet needed anything.

Ivete was already on her horse, her fishing pole in the rifle scabbard and his hat on her head. When he'd first seen her wear it, he'd not had the courage to tell her she'd stolen his finest hat. Now she'd stuck hooks through the band and it was as good as hers.

Thomas grinned at her frontier-woman image. He pointed to her crafty use of the scabbard. "Great idea." He mounted his horse and set the basket of lunch in front of him. Bastien had Della on his horse and she held a roll of fabric they would use for a shade.

Ivete beamed. "I don't know how many fish will be out this late in the day, but I can give it a go."

Thomas remembered that he had committed to fish with her this morning. "I forgot about our fishing this morning. The cow... Forgive me?"

"Of course."

Bastien led the way to the lake. Ivete's horse fell into step beside Thomas's.

He glanced at her. "How was your ride this morning?"

"It was fine. The weather is turning."

"It is. I'm afraid you may not want to ride beyond the next month."

"Oh, I think we will be back in Chicago at that time. I'm only here for a spell, to experience all that Bastien's country home has to offer. Then we will go back to the priorities of city life."

"Are you enjoying the ranch life?" He tried to focus on her. Looking away was usually impossible, but today he wished for the distraction. There was nothing to do about his finances crumbling to nothing. The best he could do was put it out of his mind and enjoy the sunshine and the beautiful woman next to him.

Once they reached the lake, Thomas came to help Della from Bastien's horse. Ivete needed no such help. The prospect of a day fishing had livened her features. The first thing she did was assemble her pole. She set off and left the rest of them to assemble the makeshift tent that would shield them from the beating sun.

When she returned, a large trout hung from her finger. "No fire?" She looked around the pebbled shore as though she'd missed it.

Bastien laughed. "I should have known you'd be back soon enough. I'll get one going."

"Oh, that is a beautiful fish." Della admired the scales but kept her distance.

Ivete smirked. "Just a little something to add to our lunch. What did Eloise pack us?"

Della ushered Ivete to the wrapped foods. "For some reason, Thomas has the largest sandwich, as though he were the one paying her wages." Della narrowed her eyes at Thomas. "I wonder ... does she fancy you?"

"She's much too young."

Della cocked her head to the side. "I wonder what her mother's thoughts about you are? If the mother fancies you as much as the girl does ..."

Thomas stepped nearer, keeping his gaze locked on Della. "I have no intentions in that direction, and I'd thank you not to go poking and prodding."

Della tossed her head. "Don't get worked up. I won't say anything if you'd prefer I don't."

"I prefer you don't." Thomas unwrapped his sandwich. The girl Eloise had lingered near him often more than once recently, bringing him small treats, staring. He knew very well she fancied him. Or at least her parents did. Afterall, they had a large family to feed, and with Mr. Morris paralysed and unable to help on the farm, the boys did everything. Eloise working for the Graham family likely brought them some financial relief, they'd want to marry her off sooner rather than later. They could look elsewhere, though. Eloise was nice, but not for him.

Thomas helped Bastien create a small fire and spit on which to cook Ivete's fish. Thomas lifted the fish to take it to the water only to find it had already been gutted. His eyes flashed to Ivete, seated near Della with her skirts pooling around her. She looked every bit the proper lady her mother trained her to be, yet she'd caught and cleaned a fish longer than her own forearm without fanfare.

He returned, flaying the fish over two sticks that would hold it out of the flames but close enough to accept the heat and smoke from the fire. When the fish was cooked, Ivete sidled her way in front of Thomas and showed him a trick to de-boning the trout. They ate their lunch, each of them quiet as they sat in the shade of the canvas.

"It's too bad the water here is too cold for swimming," Della said, her legs crossed at the ankles as she leaned back on her elbows. Her face was a picture of peace. Thomas glanced at Bastien who was smiling at his wife. It was clear his friend was pleased that Maxine suggested his wife take a few hours to herself.

"Too cold? Who told you that?" Bastien asked.

"I've felt it myself, dear. That mountain runoff is like ice on the hottest of days."

"Nonsense." Bastien stood, mischief dancing in his eyes as he cocked an eyebrow. "It may not be a Kirwin Hot Spring, but I'll take a swim right now if you wish."

"I don't wish. You'll freeze."

"*I* wish!" Ivete volunteered, a cunning smile on her face.

"Hear. Hear." Thomas sat upright, unsure if Bastien was truly going to soak himself. The sun was hot, one of the flashes of warmth that foretold the deeper cold ahead, but Della was correct. The water was freezing.

"You're not going to join me? Who will dare Thomas to jump in as well?"

"I do." Ivete laughed at Thomas's expression of shock.

Bastien grinned. "There you have it. She caught the fish. It's time to prove your grit on this expedition."

Thomas took his time climbing to his feet. He looked at

Ivete. "I didn't *try* to catch a fish. I cannot say whether you would have the lead or not."

She tossed her napkin at him and stood. "I will join you to my ankles." Squatting down, she removed her shoes and stockings.

Thomas and Bastien followed suit, dressing down to their breeches. The three started toward the shore when Bastien jogged ahead and dove into the water.

Della's gasp could be heard from the blanket.

Ivete chuckled. "Sometimes I wonder if he'll ever grow up."

"I hope not." Thomas smiled at his friend, then turned to Ivete. She flicked her eyes up to meet his, but he had seen where she'd been looking before. He resisted the urge to beat his chest like some savage. He knew he shouldn't care, but the fact that she was unable to keep up her polite manners when he was shirtless, made his heart thump in his chest.

Ivete looked out at the water. "You know, this isn't the first time I've seen you so"—she waved her hand at his frame—"indecent. If this were Chicago, I would be ruined."

Thomas bit his lips to contain his grin. "Ruined? I would have thought the way you cuddled me on that train might have spelled your end long before now."

Ivete scoffed. "I did not cuddle you, sir. You misremember. Or perhaps it was a dream." She reached out to swat him playfully on his shoulder, her mouth pulled into faux disapproval. He ignored the impulse to catch her wrist and pull her to him, and instead dodged her hand.

He had not dreamed of her as of late, but likely the reason was that he could seldom remember his dreams. Besides, what need had he of dreams when she ran through his head all day long. He shouldn't think of her as often as he did, but he could not stop.

"I must tell you," she said, lowering her voice, "this is exactly how you appear in my dreams." As soon as the words were said, she walked to the edge of the water and left him alone and rooted to the ground. Had she just ...?

"Come on!" Bastien shouted from the water, his head the only part of him that remained above the shimmering blue lake.

Ice cold water was exactly what Thomas needed. He jogged past Ivete and followed Bastien's lead, diving into the chilly water. He bobbed back to the surface, his lungs burning, his skin on fire from the cold, but feeling more alive than he had in ages. He glanced to the shore, unable to stop himself from seeking out her form.

Ivete stood in the water with her skirts tucked around her waistband. Her bare ankles and calves showed the water licking up the shore. He let himself sink under once more and turned away before he came up. As the water closed over his head, the image of Ivete appeared behind his eyes. *She dreams about me?* He came up for air, focusing on the mountain range in the distance. Why was he falling hard for a woman like Ivete? One who was terribly out of reach. He's more fit for a woman like Eloise. Why couldn't *she* be the one he wanted?

12

Water trickled from Thomas's hair and onto his bare shoulders. Ivete seemed numb to everything but that particular sight, though the water lapping at her toes stung cold. He lifted his gaze to hers and his eyes flashed to her ankles and then away before he dipped below the surface once more. She pulled her skirts higher, revealing more of her lower legs. Would more skin make him look at her in that same brazen way he had on the train and again in the stables? He'd been different then, less ... controlled. She recalled the warmth of his lips when he pressed them against hers to convince the bandit boy she was his wife. And how he'd held her close in that butler's pantry. If only she'd savored the moment instead of letting it slip away in the current of the robbery.

She turned away. Perhaps without her watchful eye trained on him, he would be unafraid to look at her more. Like a tug on a line. She didn't need to see the fish to know she wanted it. Her attention fell on Della, a beauty in her own right. It was no wonder Bastien had fallen for her. She was smart and funny as well as beautiful. Ivete tried to consider her own virtues. Beauty was praise that had been fawned on her by her friends and family, but one look at Della told Ivete what natural beauty was. Ivete's beauty was a combination of fine clothing, confidence, and wealth. If she'd possessed Della's additional beauty, would Henry have strayed?

Henry, that faithless wretch. He paled in comparison to Thomas. She'd never tried to tempt her Chicago beau with a glimpse of her ankles, but here she was, standing like a siren with her skirts almost at her knees. She knew what she wanted from Thomas, but how could she ask it of him? She'd seen the smile that the woman from the hotel had given Thomas. He must have experience beyond the kiss he'd given her during the robbery. The thought of him sleeping half-clothed snaked its way behind her eyes. She had to admit it lurked in the back of her mind at all times. If she really wanted to get back at Henry, the best plan of action would be to go to Thomas's bed. The idea churned her stomach, but it also sent a thrill shivering through her. Could she really be so bold? If only the lazy sun would head for the horizon at a quicker pace. She returned to the blanket and relaxed next to Della, watching the men splash in the water with a playfulness no respectable woman could express. Ivete thought of the conversation she'd heard between Thomas and Della. "Do you think Eloise has her sights on Thomas?"

Della shifted on the thin quilt, as if unable to get comfortable on the hard ground. "I cannot see why she wouldn't. Despite Thomas's objections, Eloise *is* of marrying age. She's more than equipped to care for a husband and children when they come along. She'd make a fine wife for him."

"Is ability what makes a fine wife?"

Della gave a small laugh and considered Ivete. "It makes for a comfortable wife. But you are right. There is much more to a marriage."

"How did you know you were right for Bastien?"

"He told me. I never thought myself worthy of him until he told me I was."

"Will you tell me of your first marriage?"

Della shook her head. "If I can, I will never speak about him again."

The silence that followed carried a weight Ivete was unsure she could bear. She was about to speak when Della broke in. "I asked Bastien to find me a husband. Sometimes I look at Thomas and wonder if he would have been my future had we stuck to the plan."

Jealousy ripped through Ivete, more potent than any she'd granted Henry's mistress or the prospect of Eloise trying for Thomas.

Della continued. "I wonder how I would have managed, living so close to Bastien and seeing him with another." Her eyes softened as they fell on her husband, and the monster within Ivete calmed. "Yet, the more I learn about Angelica, the more I doubt she would have ever made it out this far. She was right to choose Luc, and not just for my sake."

Della closed her eyes and lifted her face to the sun. "Do you doubt your compatibility with Henry?"

Ivete bit back a laugh. "I believe Henry and I are compatible in many ways. He is more than suited to a city girl, but being out here makes me wonder how *city* I really am. I always relished the time spent at my grandparent's country home. I guess I could have one of my own if I marry someone as rich as Henry."

"You will have a great many *things*." Della's voice whispered quietly between them, softening the harshness of her implication. Ivete would have *things*, but not *love*.

Ivete didn't know what to feel. Anger that a woman she'd really only just met seemed to be judging her? Or stubborn insistence that not everyone could enjoy love like Della and Bastien. But mostly, churning deep within, she fought off a gnawing and growing realization that she'd always had things and it had never been enough, a recognition that, perhaps, she didn't want things anymore. But along with that came confusion. Because who was Ivete Graham without all the things money had always bought her? It was a good thing Della didn't seem to want a response. Ivete had none, and they sat silent in the sun until the men splashed to the shore. Ivete still hadn't found words as they packed up and trekked across the long grasses toward home.

Ivete did her best to push away any thoughts of Henry and her potential future. Instead her mind wove scenarios, plotted ways to catch Thomas without getting caught by her family. As Ivete and Della rode in front and Thomas and Bastien followed, she thought of what she could do to ensure Thomas didn't toss her out of his house. As soon as that option came into her mind, she pushed it away. If Mother was right, men would dally with anything in a skirt. Yet, that doubt still hung in the back of her mind. Though she was certain he'd been with that painted woman at the hotel, part of her admitted he was different than the men her friends had experimented with. Softer, gentler. Those men were more than happy for a chance with Ivete's friends. He must possess that masculine impulse to make good on lust, to conquer any woman who bats her eyes. It was that desire Ivete wanted to awaken. If she could wake it up, she'd be more than willing to feed its hunger. But how? Hopefully showing up at his house in the middle of the night would be enough. Hopefully he'd take care of the rest.

At the barn, she waited for Thomas to help her from her horse.

"You're still wet." She pushed a lock of hair from his face and fingered the collar on his shirt, damp from his dip in the lake.

His throat bobbed, and his eyes fluttered as though they wished to close.

"Sir," a small voice came from behind the group, and Thomas stepped away from Ivete.

Eloise bobbed her head to Bastien before passing him a note. "Letter from town."

Bastien pulled his eyebrows together as he opened the letter. "From Tewksbury." His eyes roved the words, and he held the paper to Della, placing his other hand over his eyes.

Instead of reading the correspondence, Della touched Bastien's jaw. "What is it, darling?" Concern etched her face as her eyes tried to read his expression.

Ivete remembered Della's newness in reading and stepped closer. "Would you like me to read it to you?"

Della barely spared a glance for Ivete, passing her the paper and focusing once again on Bastien as she took his hand. Ivete hadn't a chance to read it before he spoke, his voice cracking. "Simon is dead. Premature explosion."

A cry escaped Della's throat, and she threw her arms around Bastien's waist. He clung to her, and Ivete stepped away from their intimacy bewildered at the sudden weight in the air.

"Come." Thomas's words were barely a whisper, but once again, the voice that pulled her away from their privacy. As they stepped through the entrance to the barn,

Ivete caught his arm, letting her hands slide down to his calloused palm and pulling him against the wall and into the corner. His confused gaze took in every point of contact between them. Ivete silently begged him to hold her as Bastien had Della. Though she'd never met this Simon, Della and Bastien's grief touched her in a way she couldn't understand. Her chest ached for a love such as theirs, no matter the effort or cost.

"Who is Simon?" she asked when no other words found their way to her lips.

"His friend from Wyoming. His wife and Della are friends, too."

Ivete stepped closer and wrapped an arm around his lean waist, inhaling his scent of peppermints and sunshine. Thomas didn't return the embrace, and when a horse knickered, he stepped away with a frown on his face. Ivete leaned into the corner and let the weight of the moment wash over her. Forget seduction. She wanted only comfort, his warm, strong arms around her, holding her like an anchor in a stormy sea. But he turned and disappeared behind the door of the stable office. Her heart caught in her throat and gooseflesh rose on her skin. Bastien and Della moved toward the house, leaving her alone. She ran to catch up.

Numb, she followed Bastien and Della into the house. Without a word, Bastien scooped Violet from their mother's arms, and the family of three retired to their bedroom.

Maxine turned stunned eyes toward Ivete. "What's happened?"

"Bastien's friend, Simon, has died. Their friend is now a widow."

"Oh." Her mother's face fell as the sadness landed on her as well.

"Eloise," Maxine called. "Bastien and Della may be

taking dinner in their bedroom tonight. Please plan accordingly."

"Yes, ma'am."

With none of the jealousy of earlier, Ivete surveyed the child, who, as Della had said, really was no child. If she had been rich in Chicago, she would have had her first season by now. As Ivete had suggested to her mother, Eloise had a touch of Della's natural beauty. The dirty calico dress didn't hide that she was young and eager.

THE ONLY SOUND at dinner that night was the clink of silverware on china. The sorrow between Bastien and Della was so thick, Ivete didn't dare cut through it with idle chatter. Maxine had tried a few times, but unsuccessfully. When Bastien did speak, Ivete jumped, unprepared to hear a voice in the silence. "I will go and see if Lydia has need of anything. I—"

"Please," Della interjected. "If you can, bring her back here. We can help with the children. I can't imagine she wants to return to her own family."

"If she has a want, I will be sure to bring her back."

"Oh, but you must do more," Della pressed. "She will not want to interfere in our life here. You must make it clear that she is not only welcome but *wanted*."

Bastien smiled at his wife with such love, Ivete's food turned to ash in her mouth. He nodded. "I would be happy to take a letter from you conveying all your wants and wishes."

Bastien turned to Thomas. "The cows will have to wait. With Harder roaming these parts, I cannot leave the women without a guardian."

Thomas gave a curt nod. "Of course."

"I hope to be back within two weeks, but if Lydia allows, I'll see her set up wherever she chooses to go. That may mean up to three weeks."

"We'll manage."

Ivete watched the interchange and was grateful that Bastien had Thomas. She wondered if Bastien would have otherwise been able to leave for his friend's funeral. His mention of Harder brought back the realization that they were at the edge of civilization. Of course people died in Chicago, but everything out here felt more real. Sharper somehow. Had she really intended to play childish games with Thomas? Such games were allowed in Chicago, but there was no place for them here. Nothing was a game out west.

13

The morning was a hustle of regular chores in addition to Bastien's preparations for departure. Thomas packed his things from the guesthouse. Everything he owned easily fit in two small packs. He didn't want to live out of a pack anymore. He wanted a sprawling home like Bastien's. Being able to carry all his belongings in a single pack felt like loneliness. But Bastien's house, big enough to fit visiting family and a bushel of children, felt like a home; felt like exactly what Thomas wanted.

An image of Thomas's floated up from his memory, swamping him in sadness. A child doesn't appreciate his mother until he's grown, and he wished he could remember more. He'd never had the chance to create those memories though. Within a year of her death, his father had found Ellen, who decided her new children needed fixing. She rarely showed love to any of them and never to Thomas. None of the children were shocked when she started pushing the older ones to move along.

A knock sounded on the doorframe of his room. He twisted to find Ivete leaning against the wall. Her small smile chased away his grim thoughts. He would miss her constant presence around the ranch once she left. He would miss the sweet surprise of her arrival throughout his days.

"All settled in?"

Thomas glanced around the room and his few belongings. "Not much to settle."

"Not compared to Mama and me." She brushed by him to sit on the bed. "It's all so sad." She slid her hand over the quilt, then pulled at one of the ties while Thomas waited for her to continue. "I realize it could have been Bastien who'd been in an accident. He did that work for nearly three years and survived. How did he miss it by less than a year?"

Thomas let out a breath. Bastien was lucky. The foreman before him had also died in a mining accident, but Thomas kept that information to himself. There was no need to upset Ivete any further. "Mining is dangerous work. That's part of why Bastien didn't continue in that field. Even managing such work conditions was something he didn't want to do."

Ivete nodded. "I thank the Lord he did."

Thomas nodded, though Ivete wasn't looking at him to see his agreement.

"Ivete?" Maxine's voice came from the hallway.

Ivete stood and gave Thomas a small smile as she breezed past him. Her familiar lilac scent lingered in the room, bringing to mind the way she'd touched his face after their trip to the lake. She'd stirred something in him he wasn't sure he could suppress. The sooner she left for Chicago, the better. Or so he tried to tell himself.

For weeks now, whenever he was out on the ranch, he found himself checking the fence line and half-expecting to see her riding toward him. When she did, a warmth grew in his chest, and he had to remind himself that she was

Bastien's sister and a woman who would marry a rich man, not one who barely had enough funds to start an endeavor.

DINNER WAS bleak without Bastien's presence. Though her eyes were no longer red-rimmed, Della remained subdued. She took the baby to bed early, and Thomas entertained Maxine and Ivete in the usual after-dinner spot near the fireplace.

Maxine broke the heavy silence. "I think we should convince your father to get another house in the country."

Ivete's voice was soft as though loudness would shatter the fragile balance. "We could visit Grandmother and Grandfather more."

Maxine tsked. "Your grandmother is too well-bred to say anything, but she does not like me there."

Ivete scoffed. "Of course she does, Mama."

Thomas relaxed into his chair. He loved when Ivete called Maxine 'Mama.' For Ivete, it was akin to a term of endearment.

"You are old enough. I don't need to shelter you anymore. Truly, I should have been helping you grow up sooner. Your grandmother isn't the first disapproving mother-in-law, and she won't be the last."

Ivete's eyes flashed to Thomas, as her cheeks flushed with embarrassment. "Mother, I am grown, whether you helped me or not. Just because I don't notice everything doesn't mean I notice nothing."

Maxine pursed her lips and didn't reply.

Ivete sighed.

Thomas tried to diffuse the argument. "A foal might be born while Bastien is away. Would either of you like to assist?"

Both women drew their heads back in a mirror gesture. The two women might not agree on much, but they were family and had more in common than they realized. Thomas laughed. "It was just a thought. I can do it myself."

Ivete drew herself higher. "I could help. If Bastien could learn, why can't I?"

Maxine answered Ivete's question, though Thomas thought it rhetorical. "You have no need to learn these things. Soon you will be married, and servants will do this filthy work."

"Mother." Ivete sent her a look of disapproval, her eyebrows drawn down and her eyes wide.

"It is different in the West. Men of all classes work hard, but back home, you'll not be more desirable for your ability to catch fish or birth foals. I daresay galavanting with farm hands will ruin your chances with anyone."

The words struck Thomas. She was right. A man like him had no place with a woman like Ivete. Besides saddling her horse, what purpose did he have with a rich woman of marrying age? Thomas stood. "I think I'll head to bed. Tomorrow is a big day."

Thomas waited until Maxine's attention drew to something else, then he cast a furtive glance at Ivete. She glared indignantly at her mother, and her annoyance warmed his heart. He smiled, a small smile Ivete did not see. Good thing, too. What need had she for a farm hand's smile?

MORNING FOUND Thomas tending stock in the barn. Mud covered almost every inch of him, and the places that were free were drenched in sweat. Maxine's words from last night echoed in his head. Filthy work. It was filthy, but someone had to do it. And why did the dirt involved make it any less valuable? "Doesn't," he grumbled, stabbing a pitchfork at the hay with more force than necessary.

"Pretending the hay is my mother?"

Thomas swung around. Ivete stood in the doorway, holding a cloth bundle, looking as clean and fresh as any pampered city lady would. The complete opposite of him. He chuckled. "Good morning."

"I'm so sorry, Thomas. My mother ... she has plans for me, and I frustrate her." She held out the cloth bundle. "These are from Eloise. She said she usually brings you breakfast."

Thomas nodded. "Thank you." When Ivete didn't immediately leave, he led her to the office and sat to eat his meal. She sat across, sadness etching her face.

"How is Della?" he asked. His friend had likely not improved much from the evening before, but he wasn't sure if Ivete's sorrow was of the same vein.

"She's fine. A bit better, I think."

"That's good news. She won't get the chance to visit Simon's grave as Bastien will. I hope it brings him comfort."

Ivete picked at a string on her skirt. "Yes. Life is short."

"Sometimes. Sometimes it is very, very long."

Her gray eyes lifted to meet his. "I wonder. When do you plan on marrying?"

Thomas inhaled, a bit of biscuit sucking back and sending him to a coughing fit. Once he could breathe without choking, he asked, "Is this about your mother wishing you to marry?"

"No. I only wonder what men do for pleasure when it takes them so long to wed."

Thomas gulped, grateful he hadn't risked another bite. Surely he would have choked once more.

When he blinked at her, unable to respond, she added, "You say you do not want Eloise, but why not? Is it because you find your needs met elsewhere, like with that woman at the hotel?"

Thomas looked around the room, his eyes and chest filling with heat. He vaguely remembered a woman at the hotel on their way here. "I am far too busy to ride into town, just for ... that. Heavens, where is this coming from?" He ran a hand over his face.

Ivete looked at him in such a way that told him she was deciding whether to tell him what was on her mind.

Without a word, she slowly rose and walked around the desk. He gulped at her proximity. At her talk of brothels. She couldn't possibly... She extended a hand and ran a finger along his hairline. Thomas briefly closed his eyes before he snapped them open and caught her wrist.

"What is this?" His voice sounded rough even to him.

"Do you not want me?"

"Want you? Ivete, your mother would be furious. Your brother ..." Thoughts of Bastien cooled his body's rising temperature, and any desire that had risen with it was dampened to its rightful place. He pushed the chair back and stood, giving her wrist a squeeze to replace the words he could not find. He took a step away, his back grazing the wall.

She laid her free hand on his chest, keeping her eyes downcast as she leaned in closer, eventually resting her forehead on his chest. "Women have wants too. It is not only the men who need satisfaction."

Releasing her hand, he gripped her shoulders so he could move around her and stalk from the office. He continued out of the barn and across the tall grasses, stopping when he reached the fence line.

Heaven help him, he hoped she would not find him! He paced as her words reverberated through him. She wanted him? He shook his head. She couldn't possibly want to throw her lot in with a man as poor as he. Her mother may have it wrong, but he wasn't much above a farm hand.

A rider crested a bluff, and Thomas shielded his eyes, trying to recognize the visitor. The lone rider had two more horses tethered, possibly pack animals. He started back, hoping Ivete had returned to the house and to safety of her mother's presence. Maybe Maxine could talk sense into her daughter before Thomas changed his mind and took Ivete at her word.

THOMAS SPENT the rest of the day worrying, about Ivete, but also about the house full of women under his care. The rider he'd seen from the fence line had served as a stark reminder—the west was not always a friendly place. Western hospitality was such that a guest at the end of the day meant a guest for the night. Not a sentiment he'd like to uphold when he had sole charge of several women and an infant.

Thomas kept away from the house and stayed busy until Eloise fetched him for supper. With a bolstering breath, he entered the house. His gaze fell on Ivete. So much for avoiding her. She met his eyes for a brief moment before training them on her plate. Guilt washed over him. He'd made her feel that shame. A woman like her should be lively and confident. Yet here she was, quiet and downcast.

"Good evening." Thomas grinned at the women in his care as if he'd never felt inappropriate desire for an inappropriate woman. "I hope you have not been waiting long. The work is greater without Bastien here."

Della smiled. "Of course. I'm glad you are here. I doubt Bastien would have left us on our own, not even for Lydia's sake."

It was Thomas's turn to burn with shame. He tried not to think what his friend would say or do if he learned what had transpired in his barn that morning.

A knock sounded on the door, and everyone exchanged glances. Eloise looked to Thomas, unsure as to whether she should go and open it. Thomas scooted his chair backward with a screech and tossed his napkin on the seat. "I'll get it, Eloise." Maybe it was whomever he'd seen riding along the fence line earlier. His heart raced. He tried to calm it. No need for that. He had no idea who was at the door, but his thoughts from earlier about unwelcome guests wouldn't move on. He opened the door.

"Hello, old friend." Aaron Harder leaned against the door frame, looking relaxed but ready at the same time, a silly grin on his face.

Thomas's throat closed up, his hold on the door tightened.

"No embrace? We can't have that." Aaron opened his arms and wrapped Thomas in a crushing hug topped with a hearty slap on the back. "This isn't your place, is it? The folks in town told me you were working here, not that you owned it."

Thomas crossed his arms and leaned against the door-frame. "Not mine. I've partnered with Mr. Graham. We're trying to start a horse breeding business."

"Ah, yes. That explains the excellent mounts I've brought to you."

Thomas narrowed his eyes while his friend whistled

over his shoulder. Another man came around the corner leading none other than the three mounts stolen from the train.

Thomas lifted his brows. Aarron Harder was bringing back his horses. Miracles never ceased. Or was it a trick in disguise?

"At first, I thought one of our kids was selling me a story, but when he said your name, I knew he must have been tellin' it true. Says you've got yourself a wife." Aaron stretched his neck toward the door as though he could catch a glimpse of this fictitious wife.

"Yes, well ..." After such a long day, Thomas's mind couldn't keep up. Should he tell Aaron the truth? Though the danger from that train ride was long gone, Harder's sudden appearance didn't sit well with Thomas. "Thank you for returning my horses. How did you know they were mine? It's not like I handed them over to your boys. The beasts were back in the cattle car."

"Ah, that was a bit of a mystery. I had to speak with a gentleman in the train office who went over the manifest. I was sad to learn that roan was yours. Hope you don't mind. I rode her a few times, and boy"—he whistled appreciatively —"is she tall."

"Yes." *And not yours to ride.* Thomas swallowed his retort.

"Aren't you going to invite me in? My man can get these beasts settled in the barn. I was hoping for a bit of Western hospitality from my old friend. Whatever is cooking in there smells mighty nice."

Thomas's shoulders tightened. He couldn't let one of Harder's men into Bastien's stable. He'd be asking for trouble, and possibly one less horse come morning. But what option did he have? He knew just how dangerous Harder's gang was. He didn't want to find out what his men would do if denied a little Western Hospitality.

"I've got one mare who's just given birth. She's a bit skittish. Let's go together to get these mounts settled. Then I'd be happy to have you in for supper. Let me just see if we can't provide a bit for your men as well. How many did you say there were?"

Aaron smirked. There was a time when Aaron knew Thomas's mind as well as Thomas himself. Thomas's old friend always was sharp, and he didn't work his way up to leading a gang without sniffing out a pretense or two. "Twelve altogether," Harder said, "but they've beans and biscuits. No need to waste whatever your girl's got in there."

Thomas twisted to follow Harder's eyes as they moved to something behind him. Della had come around the corner, her face laced with confusion. "Thomas?"

Harder whistled, low, appreciatively.

Thomas groaned inwardly. "Della, this is my old friend—"

Harder stepped over the threshold, reaching his hand out to Della. "Aaron Harder. Pleased to meet you, ma'am."

Thomas clenched his jaw. As much as he hated seeing Harder on Bastien's doorstep, he hated more the sight of the man inside Bastien's house, leering at his wife. Thomas hadn't invited Harder in. He didn't want him in, but his *friend* often did as he pleased. Della stepped forward and offered her hand. Aaron bowed over it like an English lord, pressing his lips to her knuckles before releasing it.

Thomas stepped between the pair. "He has a few men outside. Can you see if Eloise can find anything to feed them? Also, can we set another place at the table for my friend? He's returned our missing broodmares, and we're going to set them up in the barn. Back shortly."

"Yes." Della spun and trotted back toward the kitchen.

Once she was out of sight, Thomas let out a breath.

Had Della read the situation right? He couldn't say a word in front of Harder, but maybe she knew him well enough to sense his unease.

"Shall we?" Thomas lifted an arm to usher Harder outside and fell into step with him as they made their way to the barn.

Aaron shoved his hands into his trouser pockets. He glanced over his shoulder at the house as if trying to get a final look at Della. "She's a beaut. No wonder my men tried to take her from the train. Surprised they didn't take her for themselves."

Thomas's stomach twisted at the prospect of any woman being subject to such treatment. With a deep breath, he tried to push away the thought that some girl had likely replaced the role those men had planned for Ivete.

"You been in the area long? Thought I saw a rider earlier today. Was that you?"

"Suppose it was one of my men."

One of Harder's men led the horses to stand in front of the barn. Thomas looked over his clothes—dusty from travel, but good quality. He opened the door and led both bandits to the empty stalls at the end. May as well let coyotes into the henhouse. Thomas breathed slowly, working hard to hide his rising fears. They placed the horses inside and gave each animal a bit of dinner before exiting the barn. Thomas stamped out the urge to lock the doors, one didn't offend Harder's gang without consequences.

"Saw a little house yonder. Don't suppose you'd put me up for the night?"

"As I said, this isn't my place. Mr. Graham owns it. I don't suppose he'd be opposed to you staying one night, seeing as how you've returned our mares and turned our breeding venture around. I was sad to see those three go."

"Let me tell you. I'm sad to see them go, too. Suppose you sell me the first colt from that roan?"

Thomas forced a laugh but didn't meet Harder's eyes. *Suppose Bastien doesn't want to sell a colt to a bandit.* "I'll see what I can do." He began to sweat as they neared the house. Was he really bringing Harder inside? He took a calming breath, thankful that at least Bastien had a guest house and he could lock up the doors of the main house when they went to sleep.

IVETE'S FOOD rested untouched on her plate. What were they doing out there? Who was at the door?

When Della stormed into the room, all eyes swept to her. She stood, head cocked. Listening? For what? The sound of the front door clicking closed in the next room seemed to jolt Della into action, and she turned to Eloise.

"There are several men outside. They need a bit of whatever we can scrounge up to feed them." She lifted her eyes to Ivete and Maxine. "The man at the door is the leader of the gang who stole our horses and held up your train."

Ivete's eyes flashed to her sister-in-law. "Thomas's friend?"

"Yes." Della turned to Eloise again. "You will have to wait to get escorted home. You may need to sleep here tonight. I'll not let you traverse the distance with men like this filling our yard."

Eloise gave an anxious nod, and both women got to work gathering food for the additional mouths.

Her mother leaned across the table, gripping Ivete's wrist. "Thomas is friends with a horse thief?"

Ivete's throat was tight with worry. Thomas was out there now with that dangerous man. "*Old* friends. He said they haven't seen much of each other these past eight years, and the man—I believe his name is Harder—is a threat. We must take care, Mama."

"Of course."

Della slid a basket over her arm. "Eloise and I will deliver these."

Ivete's throat dried up. She didn't want anyone going out there, not without Thomas by their side. She cursed Bastien for leaving at such an inopportune time, for building his life in a place so wild his family wasn't safe without his constant presence.

Maxine and Ivete watched the hallway that led to the front door in stunned silence as they counted the minutes until the two women returned. When Della and Eloise finally entered, they heaved a communal sigh.

Della met Ivete's gaze. Unease was clear on her face, from her tight lips to her wide eyes, but Della returned to her seat as Eloise laid out another place setting.

Maxine spoke, her voice strong. "Ivete, move down one so Thomas can sit next to his friend."

Ivete did as she was told, her body thrumming with the prospect of danger. She felt like bolting for the door, hiding in her room. But her mother, sitting calm and tall and barking orders, set an admirable example to follow. Ivete steeled her spine and waited.

None of them moved as they waited for the two men to join their table.

Ivete glanced at Della. "Thomas says Harder is dangerous."

Della's throat bobbed. She nodded, her eyes darkening with more worry. She stood and lifted Violet from where she lay asleep on the armchair nearest the table, cradling her close. The front door sounded, and deep voices carried into the house.

Thomas led Harder inside the house, his stomach clenching with concern. If only he could have had a moment alone with the women before seating a wolf at their table.

As they entered the dining area, the women stared, their eyes as wide as the dinner plates before them. Della held Violet, pulling the babe tighter when Harder's eyes fell on her again.

Thomas cleared his throat. "This is my old friend. He's brought the stolen mares back to us. Turns out I didn't fill out that manifest for nothing." Thomas took Bastien's usual seat at the head of the table, leaving Harder to sit next to Ivete. The snake's proximity to innocent Ivete caused his throat to go dry. He ran damp palms down his pants and resolved to keep one eye on Harder throughout the meal.

Harder grinned wide. "Evenin', ladies. I apologize for having interrupted your supper. I'm much obliged for letting me join your table."

"Of course," Della said, her tone hovering between cautious and welcoming.

Harder sat, and Thomas made introductions. "This is Della Graham. Her husband owns this ranch and is off helping to bury a friend. Mrs. Graham is her mother-in-law, and last we have Ms. Ivete Graham, her daughter."

"All Grahams? But where is Mrs. McMullin? I was

hoping that one was yours." He nodded at Della. "And you had yourself a brat as well."

A muscle in Della's jaw flickered, and Thomas silently cursed his friend's tactlessness. Too long in the company of men.

Thomas cleared his throat. "No wife for me. I might have bent the truth a bit to get your boy to release his booty."

Harder gave a hearty laugh and slapped the table.

The women jolted in their seats.

Harder never noticed their discomfort. Or didn't care. "High and mighty Thomas McMullin, telling lies."

The nickname grated on Thomas. Was it high and mighty to make an honest living? To love a woman for her heart rather than steal her from her mother on a train? He swallowed those words, walking the line between lies and truth. Had he offended Harder or amused him? It was often difficult to tell. Just to be safe, he had to think quickly, to justify the lie that might push his former friend into a dangerous rage. He prayed Ivete would play along. "Well, not married yet, but soon enough. I couldn't very well let your men sneak off with my intended simply because a few months stand between us and the titles of husband and wife."

Harder pointed his fork at Ivete. "This one?"

"Yep." Thomas trained his eyes on Maxine. Ivete would understand the danger she was in, but Maxine might blow their story wide open.

She gave the smallest of nods. She accepted the ruse.

His shoulders relaxed a degree.

Aaron pointed his fork at Ivete. "When is the wedding? I don't expect to be your best man, but I'd like to see this one all dolled up and putting your mug to shame."

Ivete blushed and looked at her lap.

Thomas opened his mouth, but before he could fumble an answer, Maxine interjected. "Spring, of course. One cannot marry without flowers. Are you married, Mr ...?"

"Harder. Aaron Harder. Your soon-to-be son-in-law and I grew up together back in Livingston. We had ourselves a few adventures. I was hoping to recruit him on a few more." Aaron laughed, the noise echoing across the silent table as though his every word weren't a veiled threat. He stabbed his fork into the meal, king of the mountain, just like the game they played as kids. Except this wasn't sport. Della hadn't loosened her hold on Violet, and Ivete's porcelain skin was verging on chalk white.

14

Ivete listened to the table conversation as though hearing the words through a closed window. When Thomas mentioned being intended to Ivete, she had to forcibly glue her mouth shut to avoid ruining Thomas's plan.

As the sun dipped below the horizon, Ivete wondered if Eloise would be heading home today or staying the night. The thought of sleeping while danger prowled so near made Ivete's heart thump. She glanced at her mother. They should sleep together.

Harder ate more than twice what anyone at the table consumed, including Thomas, and Eloise's hand shook as she dished him more food. The girl would faint if pressed upon him much longer.

Thomas cleared his throat. "Della, I ask your permission for my friend to use the guest house tonight." Thomas made a slow fist on the table and pulled his gaze from Della to stare at Ivete. Something troubling lurked behind his eyes. As soon as she saw it, it disappeared, replaced by the cool demeanor he'd shown the day of the robbery.

"Of course." Della's grace in the face of such frightening

circumstances was unmatched. Harder would have no idea she suspected anything.

Della's words acted like a release. The men stood and left for the door as the women cleared the table.

The second the door closed, her mother hurried to Ivete's side. "Why did he say you were intended?" Her whisper hissed sharply between them.

Ivete dropped her hands and stared at the ceiling. When she looked back at her mother, she let out a slow breath. "When he saved me from the bandits on the train, he told them I was his wife."

When it looked like her mother was about to object, Ivete added, "It was the only way he could convince them to let me go."

Her mother nodded, staring at the sink in thought. Then she sighed and met Ivete's eyes. "We must continue this ruse." She took Ivete by the shoulders. "You must be smart, Ivete. Follow Thomas's lead. I trust he knows how to handle this man."

Did her mother truly think she would do something stupid? She sighed. Best not to argue about that now. Rather, she'd never thought to hear her mother compliment Thomas, and this might be as close as she got to it. She savored it, then turned back to the dishes.

Thomas returned, striding across the room toward Eloise. He placed a hand on her shoulder, looking every bit like a knight in shining armor. "Gather your things. I'll see you and Otto off the property."

Della stepped forward. "But can they not spend the night?"

Thomas shook his head. "I'll not endanger anyone else's life. They can return when Harder has been gone a few days." Thomas's gaze flicked to the mounted gun hung above the front door and back to Della. "Do you know how to work that?"

She recoiled from Thomas and stammered. "N-no."

Ivete stepped forward. "I do."

Thomas started at her admission.

She shrugged. "Years of hunting with three brothers. Does it have bullets?"

Thomas pulled it down and checked. "Yes." He passed it to Ivete. Eloise appeared, her face white as a dead pig.

With a nod, Thomas led the girl from the house, and once again, the silence pressed on the women like a heavy quilt.

Her mother's mouth twisted, deepening the wrinkled grooves around her mouth. "He leaves us unprotected to take that girl home. I told you she was too pretty for a maid." She cast a knowing look at Della.

Something flashed in Della's eyes and her jaw flexed. She turned from the older woman and busied her hands with wiping the table.

Della clearly didn't agree, but Ivete did. She felt Thomas's absence on a physical level, as if she were standing in the middle of a wide, open plain during a storm. She was vulnerable. Eloise had his protection now. And it was her job to protect the others. "Why don't we double up beds tonight?"

Della's face softened as she glanced at Ivete. "Violet is up at all hours. Anyone who sleeps with me will not get any rest."

Ivete's mother stepped forward to touch Violet's cheek. "My room is next to yours. Surely we would hear anyone cry out?"

Ivete nodded. "Yes. May I sleep with you, Mama?"

The women hurried down the hall with the quiet stealth

of wild animals. When she opened the door to her mother's room, Ivete half-expected to find a man waiting to attack. Once she checked every corner, she and her mother helped each other undress.

After sliding on a nightgown of her mother's, both women went to check on Della. She was nursing Violet in the rocking chair.

Ivete sat on the bed. "I'm sorry Bastien is gone. This timing is terrible."

"I do wish he was here, but Lydia needs him now. She doesn't have anyone to care for her. The least I can do is lend what I have."

"Do you need anything?"

"Just for Thomas to return."

Ivete nodded. She had no idea the time it would take to deliver Eloise and Otto to the property line. Once again, she tried to subdue the sliver of jealousy that worked its way into her core. A small huff of laughter escaped her lips. Just the other day, she'd been carefree and dipping her feet in the lake. She'd made a plan to seduce Thomas in his house. Those foolish ideas now seemed further away than ever before. Now, she was too scared to venture to her room for a nightgown, let alone across the lawn to a man's lodgings.

The door to the bedroom inched open and her mother slipped through. "When do you expect Thomas to return?"

Della chewed her lip. "I am unsure."

"You don't think he would go to the authorities?" Ivete whispered.

"He hasn't shared his plans with me."

The women tucked their legs into Della's bed and leaned against the headboard. Ivete stared at Violet, asleep in her cot and unaware of the danger that pulsed all around them.

She'd begun to doze, her chin on her chest, when a

sound came from the front of the house. Della, in the middle, reached for Ivete and Maxine's hands, gripping them with a fierceness only a mother possessed.

Maxine slid from between the covers. None of the women spoke. Maxine lifted a lantern from the table and gave a grim nod. She straightened her back before striding for the door. For all of her mother's propriety, Ivete had to admit she was brave.

"Wait!" Ivete whisper-yelled. "I have the gun." She climbed out of the safety of Della's blankets and followed her mother. When they reached the kitchen they could hear shuffling near the front door.

Her mother lifted the lantern higher so the light cast on the plank floor. "Thomas?" she called into the darkness beyond.

"It's me." Thomas's voice was heavy, tired.

Ivete lowered the rifle so the end of the long barrel touched the ground, and squeezed her mother's free hand.

Thomas came around the corner, scrubbing his drawn, haggard face. He looked as if a single night had aged him several years.

His return created a strange sensation in Ivete. She had little time to identify it because a rush of adrenaline quickly overtook it. The urge to shout and slap him almost overcame her. Thomas reached for the gun, slipping it from Ivete's weak grip.

Her mother took Thomas's arm. "Will we be safe tonight?"

"I dearly hope so. The one thing that is for sure is, I cannot predict Harder's intentions."

Ivete gulped. "How many are with him?"

"He said twelve. I figure at least a few more." He lay the gun over his shoulder, like a peddler's pack.

"I'm going to ask you, ladies, to sleep with your doors open. I'll make a pallet right outside." He pointed to the hallway.

Her mother turned and bustled down the hall.

Ivete's legs wouldn't move. Anger and fear had rooted her to this spot. She flicked her gaze to Thomas. His face softened and he set the gun next to the lantern, stepping closer. "Are you okay?"

Ivete took a shaky breath. "No, I'm not okay." She wondered how he could ask such a question. Her body was pulsing with fear, adrenaline...and jealousy. She pressed her fists against his chest. He stood as strong as a tree, her efforts did little to sway him. She tried again, pushing harder. Then she beat at his chest. "You ran off with Eloise." Hit. "When your duty is to—" She swallowed the word *me* and continued, "Della." Hit. "Bastien is your employer; your loyalty is to *him*, not some pretty girl from down the lane."

Thomas caught her wrists as they beat at his chest, punctuating her words. She tried to wrench free but only caused herself to stumble into him. He wrapped his arms around her, not letting go when she struggled against him.

A sob broke from her throat and Ivete cried into his chest, "Why did you choose *her*?" She relaxed against him, her anger spent. In the quiet aftermath of her outburst Ivete heard a door close down the hall. She pushed away from him again. This time he let her go. She looked at him with guarded eyes, the hurt still sharp in her chest.

"I didn't *choose* her. The Morrises are my responsibility too."

He wasn't even sorry. She hated the fact that he didn't see his error. That if he were to do it all over again, he would still leave Ivete here with a gun in her hands and two women and a baby in her charge.

"And what if something had happened. Could you live with yourself after you left us?"

"If anyone is hurt due to Aaron's hand, I'll never forgive myself for bringing him down on this ranch. Be it Morris, or Graham, I'll not be able to forgive myself."

"You left us." Ivete's voice was weak, her anger ebbing and fatigue setting in.

Thomas took her hand and interlaced his fingers with hers. "I rode like hell to get back to you."

Ivete fisted his shirt and laid her head on his chest. He wrapped his arms around her and she didn't want him to ever let go.

An infant's wail came from the back rooms, and Thomas released her. Ivete glanced at her attire and flushed at his embrace when she was dressed only in a nightgown. She made her way down the hall to find her mother completing a bed in the hallway.

"Where have you been? I used all of Della's blankets."

Ivete heard the shuffle of Thomas's feet as he joined them in the hallway. Her mother's eyes lifted to his. "It's no feather mattress..."

"I won't be getting much sleep anyway." Thomas set the lantern on a side table and leaned the rifle against it as well.

Ivete stepped over the makeshift bed, closer to the bedrooms. "My mother and I are sharing her bed."

Thomas nodded. "That's good. Safer." His eyes scanned the hallways as though searching for unseen danger.

Her mother touched her arm and Ivete followed her into the bedroom.

As they settled in, Ivete stared at the ceiling in the darkness. She could hear quiet movements out in the hallway. She must be mad because she wanted to laugh at Thomas sleeping outside her bedroom door. Only days ago she would have been thrilled at the prospect. Now her mother was laying next to her, the option had never been further away. Her mind drifted to her reaction, shocking in it's revelation. Had she truly been angry at Thomas for choosing Eloise, or were her tears to do with Henry's lover?

She thought of Della, with a baby to protect. Yet she hadn't voiced any displeasure at Thomas's decision. Della had understood Thomas's need to escort Eloise and Otto home. It was Mother's words that had inflamed Ivete's jealousy. Funny how those two women had such different marriages. Della had a faithful husband, and mother did not. Could such a thing translate into other aspects of her life? If Ivete married Henry, would she become bitter at other men for choosing pretty maids, or protecting pretty maids? Would the pain of being put on a shelf leak into other areas of her life?

BY THE TIME the sun's warm rays sliced across her eyes, prodding her awake, Ivete's every limb drooped as though covered in thick Montana mud. Della was right. Violet *had* been up at all hours. She braided her hair into a simple plait down her back, too tired to do anything more.

"How have you made it through these weeks? Are you getting *any* sleep?"

Della smiled. "As you know, I rest during the day. This girl does what she wants, and there's no reasoning with her."

Ivete's mother lifted a brow, a sly smile on her lips. "They don't change as they get older."

Ivete laughed and wound an arm around her mother's

waist. "I promise to be more reasonable if we make it through this man's visit."

The spot where Thomas slept was empty and his bedding folded into a pile along the wall. The women made their way to the kitchen. Della gave orders as they readied the ingredients to make enough biscuits to feed Harder's small army.

While Ivete was cutting circles in the dough, Della stood at her elbow. "You're doing great. We want to get them close, so we don't have to roll out the dough too many times. These are the best tasting ones." She took a piece of dough and popped it in her mouth. "The other ones have too much flour."

Ivete tried a bit of the raw dough and made a face. She looked at the flour-covered counter. How could a dusting of flour alter the taste? Flour was a bit like money, wasn't it. You needed it to create something of substance, but too much of it and the goodness began to dwindle.

Once they'd been in the kitchen for almost two hours, they each slid a basket onto their arm and made for the guest house. Della knocked with more purpose and confidence than Ivete possessed.

Harder finally answered, tucking his shirt into his pants and using the same hand to wipe his nose. "Ain't you a sight for sore eyes. What can I do you for?"

Della lifted her basket. "We brought breakfast for you and your men. You're welcome to take the towels. I know how Mr. Graham hates crumbs in his saddlebag."

Ivete suppressed a smile at Della's veiled suggestion they be off her property.

"I thank you. I'll be sending my men back today, but I wondered if you wouldn't mind me staying yet another night. I have some business to discuss with Thomas."

A chill ran its creeping fingers up Ivete's spine. What business did this slimy bandit have with Thomas?

Della's voice ran like warm honey. "We would enjoy your company at our table for another evening." She set her basket down on the step, and Ivete and Maxine followed suit. "Good day." Della nodded and led the two women away.

Except for a stop at the chicken coop to gather eggs, the three women spent the entirety of the morning in the kitchen. In the late afternoon, Maxine pointed out the window. "Look. Riders, and they're headed away from the house. Harder's men, hopefully."

Della sat for the first time that day, a huff of exhaustion leaking out of her. "A blessed relief. Now just to get Harder on his way." She yawned, her mouth opening bigger than the biscuits she made.

Ivete took her by the elbow and ushered Della down the hall. "Off to bed with you."

Eventually, Maxine fell asleep with the baby in her arms, her head resting on the cushions. Ivete was torn between fatigue and anxiousness. Where was Thomas? She'd not seen him all day. What was he up to with Harder? Was he lying dead in a field because he had rejected his friend for the last time?

She paced the house, attempted to knead a bit of Della's bread dough, and swept the floors. She almost smiled to think how shocked her old self would be to see her doing these chores. When she could think of nothing else to fill her time or absorb her anxious energy, she found the hat she'd taken from the office and plunked it on her head, then marched to the barn. She checked the office first. No Thomas. A lump rose in her throat as she searched the stalls. One stall remained. With trembling fingers, she pushed open the door. Thomas blinked up at her, and she threw herself into his arms. "I thought he'd hurt you."

Thomas stroked her hair. "Hurt me? Darling, he's my oldest friend."

The pet name gave Ivete pause, and she hid her face for a moment to gather her wits. Harder must be within earshot.

"I know, but they say the west is so wild." She released him and cast her eyes around the stall. Harder wasn't in sight, but if Thomas was playing the game, she would too.

"Are you wanting to take your ride?"

"Heavens, no. I daresay I'll not ride alone again." She rubbed her arms, cold where they no longer held Thomas.

A deep drawl came from the stall next to theirs. "You sure you wanna bet your money on this one?" Harder crept around the corner and stuck his thumb at Thomas. "There are plenty of men in this wild west looking for a nice lady like yourself. Richer too."

Thomas cast an irritated eye toward Harder.

Ivete's spine stiffened. "My brother tells me there's a surplus of men looking for wives, but I know better than most that money does not make a good husband." She stepped closer to Thomas, letting her arm rub against his in solidarity. "I am marrying for other reasons."

Once voiced, the idea exploded in her mind, filling every corner. Of course, she should marry for other reasons. It was an idea that started growing the moment she'd learned of Henry's betrayal. Someone like Della might have been raised to believe such things. Ivete, however, had been taught differently. Appearance. Power. Money. These were the things to be admired in their social circles. Thomas possessed none of those things in the Chicago way, yet he had everything that counted out west.

He was shaggy and unkempt, sure, with stubble on his jaw and dirt on his clothes, but he had more raw muscle than any man she'd met in Chicago, and his wheat blonde hair and moss-green eyes were enough to make any Chicago maiden flutter her eyelashes in welcome. He may not have power over men like Harder, but his ability to walk the line with his rogue friend was impressive. Harder was right; Thomas had no money, but Bastien trusted him and listened to his advice regarding their shared business. Ivete didn't doubt that over time, Thomas would see himself quite comfortable.

Ivete slid her hand into his, weaving her fingers with his calloused ones and for the first time seeing him as a friend and not a pawn to ease her wounded pride. The words she'd spoken to Harder echoed in her ears. Could she truly marry for other reasons? And if she did, would he have her? She couldn't help the twinge of embarrassment she felt at the thought of telling her friends back home of her choice. If they thought her foolish for ending things with Henry, they'd call her mad for choosing a man with nothing but two satchels to his name.

15

Ivete's hand was as smooth as a pearl when she pressed it into his. Thomas gave her a small squeeze to show his appreciation for her words. If only they were real and not spoken to convince Harder.

"I can tell she's infatuated with you. Am I interrupting your usual romp in the hay?" Harder whipped his head around as though searching for such a place.

Thomas took a step toward Harder, but Ivete yanked his arm. Thomas met her eyes and shook his head, releasing her hand.

He stepped nose-to-nose with Harder. "You are a guest, and I'll not have anyone insulting Ivete in that manner."

Harder laughed and threw his hands in the air. "We've both come a long way from sharing Missy Jones." He returned to the stall where he was cleaning out the horse's hooves.

Thomas turned back to Ivete. "Back to the house." His voice was rough and blood pounded in his ears despite Harder's surrender.

When Ivete didn't move, Thomas snatched her hand

and tugged her out of the barn and across the tall grass. When they reached the front porch, he stopped and searched her face, his eyes filling with concern. "Any encounter with Harder isn't safe. *Please*, don't look for us again."

"I was looking for *you*. I wanted to be certain you were safe."

"I'm not safe. Not while he is here. But your presence only makes it worse."

Ivete placed both hands on his chest. Rising on her toes, she said, "Kiss me."

Thomas wanted to laugh at the idea, but instead, her proximity made him swallow. She fisted his shirt and pulled him closer. Her hot breath whispered along his jaw. Finally, he dipped down and pressed his lips against her. His hands wound around her back and pulled her tighter.

Too soon, she lowered herself down and away from him. In his chest, his heart thundered. Should he apologize? She'd requested the kiss, but she'd also pulled away first. That was no quick, chaste kiss like he'd given her that day outside the train. Her chest rose and fell in quick breaths, and her eyes held an emotion he couldn't identify.

As though she didn't want him to read her, she dropped her gaze and went inside. Once the door closed, Thomas leaned his head against the door frame. What would Bastien think? He raised his hand to wipe away the kiss, but instead, he held it there, pressing in the taste of her lips.

HARDER LAUGHED WHEN THOMAS RETURNED. "Gotta be hard living so close to a girl who won't give herself to you."

Thomas glared at his old friend.

"Shoulda let my boys bring her to me. I coulda taught her a thing or two then passed her back."

"Aaron, don't press me." Thomas shot him a look that was harder than steel.

Harder's words were crass, but without Ivete to hear them, Thomas let them slide. He thought of the day of the train robbery, and what it would have done to Ivete to have been taken to Harder. The image fueled a rage inside Thomas and he met his friend's gaze straight on, not caring whether any offense was given. "What would your mama say?"

Doubt crossed Harder's face for a moment before he chased it away. "I reckon she's glad of the money I send her."

"And what about when it stops?"

Harder leaned against the wall, crossing his ankles. "I'll keep caring for her as long as I live."

"Exactly." Thomas waited, letting his meaning fall into place. "Robbing banks and trains is one thing. Kidnapping and raping women ... they won't allow that to continue. If they haven't already, they're going to bring out every bounty hunter this side of the Mississippi."

The smirk disappeared from Harder's face. "Hangin' ain't what I expected when I started, but I know well enough it's the end I'll meet. Live big, die soon."

"What will your mama do once you're gone?" The words were spoken with the intent to sober his old friend. A futile wish Thomas had thought long gone cut through him. No matter the time or the changes to Aaron, Thomas still wished he'd set aside his dishonest ways, settle down like they'd planned. Only, now that was a dream Aaron could never make into reality. Not with his face hanging in every post office from here to California.

"Why d'you think I brought you those mares? I may not

have lived the life we planned, but you're living fancy. You know she thinks of you as a second son. Couldn't hurt to send her some money now and then."

Thomas did know. "I'll never forget how she took me in after Ellen threw me out, you know that. She's like a second mother to me, more so even than my stepmother."

Harder laughed. "Ellen isn't exactly a beacon of motherliness. She threw you out quick as a summer storm comes and goes."

"Of course, I'll help her out. I'm not making much yet. The cows keep falling to some sickness. But I hope to start."

"I have a fair bit of gold in that guesthouse. I don't suppose you'd accept any?"

"Stolen? No." The answer came too fast, and Thomas wished he'd at least pretended to consider. "Why not just give it right to your mama?"

Aaron toed the ground as he shook his head. "Isaac lives next door. He'd drink or gamble away anything I sent her." Aaron lifted his gaze to meet Thomas's. "What if it weren't a gift, but an investment? I set you up now, so you can take care of Mama while I'm gone."

Thomas clapped his friend on the shoulder. "Can't you stop? Cut your losses and leave the table."

Harder shook his head. "You said it yourself. Every bounty hunter from the Mississippi to the golden coast knows my face. Even if I grow a beard, I'll never live a normal life." He scratched at his whiskers as though considering the thought.

Thomas wished he could have forced his old friend to join him those eight years ago, instead of leaving him with the band. He should have dragged Aaron away from that flashy life that led to a noose.

Thomas dropped his hand and stood next to Aaron, mirroring his position against the wall.

"You think it's coming?" The end. The noose. "That's why you're making arrangements?"

"I shoulda left a long time ago. The gang knows I'm not going back, but it's too late for the rest of the world. I'll never fade into obscurity."

"Not going back? You *are* done?"

Harder gave a solemn nod.

Too bad he'd waited too long to quit. The silence stretched, and Thomas was torn between pity for his friend and a sense of justice.

Aaron's voice was a notch above a whisper. "You know, I never raped or kidnapped. That was Rogers's doing. I told him to bring me something pretty, I meant a nice sack of gold or fine jewelry, and he knew it." Harder shook his head. "Rogers is a dark fellow. I fear under his leadership the gang will turn into something else entirely."

"Why are you leaving? You're so certain of your death, yet you're still going to try to live in obscurity?"

"I've grown sober in my old age. A year of quiet solitude would be nice."

A year would be a gift indeed, but Harder hadn't earned any peace and he likely wouldn't get it. Nevertheless... "I hope you get it."

"So you'll take my gold? Let me help you get started? You can stop working for this guy and build a ranch of your own."

"I'll finish out my contract. Take my pay and see what I can do."

"Plus, you don't want to upset your future brother-in-law."

Guilt flickered in Thomas's chest. Though they were

the same age, down to the month, the last several years had made Harder seem older, wizened. Without his bravado, Harder didn't seem so much the threat as he had last night.

"Maybe when you get a place of your own, I can help out." Aaron shot him a look of hope. "I'll give you seed money and my labor so long as I'm breathing."

Thomas's chest ached at the prospect. That had been their plan from the start, to make enough money to start a ranch together. Build two houses on the property and raise their kids as cousins. But Harder had ruined everything. Thomas's plan was to build a ranch where his siblings could seek shelter. He wanted a safe place to build a life. And yet, hadn't Mrs. Harder taken Thomas in when she could barely afford to feed her own children? He might not be able to send her money, but the least he could do would be to help her son during his final days.

"My contract is over in June. If you are truly done with thieving, you find me then, and we'll see what we can create."

Aaron nodded. Stepping away from the wall, he offered a hand to Thomas and they shook as Aaron pulled him in to slap his back. "You keep an eye out for a pretty girl for me. Looks like you've got them aplenty."

Thomas watched the silhouette of Aaron's retreating frame as he left the stable. Thomas shook his head at his foolhardy invitation. No matter the funds he might contribute, Aaron helping Thomas ranch might bring the authorities into his sphere. Might bring any member of those bandits to his doorstep. But Aaron was on his way off this ranch; wasn't that everything Thomas had wanted from the moment he saw his old friend's face? He could deal with the consequences at another time. Maybe a time when he didn't have three dear women who were depending on him for their safety.

"He's gone," Thomas announced at dinner.

A chorus of sighs arose around the table.

Maxine leaned back in her seat, the breath leaving her in a whoosh. "I'll be glad to have Eloise back."

Ivete cast a sidelong look at her mother. "You did *so* much today."

Maxine either missed or ignored the sarcasm. "We all did. Della, I can*not* believe you worked so hard before we got Eloise for you."

Della smiled demurely, but her eyes danced with amusement. "She's been a great help."

Thomas winced. "I don't think we should call her back right away. I want Harder and his men good and gone before we bring anyone back to this ranch."

Ivete's voice was small. "Is there still danger?" Her pleading eyes tugged at his chest. He sat on his hands, fighting the urge to take hers and lend comfort.

"A little more than there always is. Their gang is nothing to take lightly. I don't want Eloise moving between our ranches, and I don't want anyone else in their crossfire."

"How long?" Maxine's tone was miserable, but from the looks Della and Ivete had given her, she wasn't the one doing Eloise's work.

"Three, maybe four days?"

Both Maxine and Ivete's jaws dropped.

"Also, keep your eyes peeled for any riders in this valley. Come to me directly if you see one. I don't care how far off."

The somber group ate their meal in silence. Afterward,

Thomas sat by the fire. He couldn't help but circle his thoughts around a deep glass of brandy from Bastien's cupboard. The memory of Ivete's kiss haunted him, chasing away any notion he might have had that Bastien wouldn't begrudge him a drink.

Harder leaving was good in more ways than one. That ruse was foolish and no longer necessary. As he stared into the flames, he thought of his conversation with his old friend. Had the man really changed? Thomas drew in a breath and raised his eyebrows. He might find out in June if Harder was truly intent on helping Thomas start his ranch. Might give his friend a brief respite from what the world planned to give him.

16

Ivete left Thomas to glare at the fire and readied for bed. Thomas was especially silent after their meal, and the stress of the day had worn her out.

She woke with a gasp, having dreamt of Thomas again. She lay in bed, calming her breathing, but it was no use, not when she could so easily recall the way he'd pulled her tight for their kiss. Any doubts she may have had in regards to his affection were assuaged. If that kiss was any indication, he wanted her as badly as she wanted him.

She shouldn't seduce him. But she wanted to. No, he was no pawn in some game between her and Henry. But he was the man she wanted. Desperately. And now that she knew he wanted her to, she could not silence her desire. And her realization that he was a worthy man and not a nameless pawn only made that desire deeper. She didn't just want a warm male body. She wanted Thomas—his heart, his mind, his courage, his intellect, and, yes, his body, too.

That was it. She threw the quilt off her and stood. She couldn't go another second without seeing him, without finding out just how much he returned her feelings.

The room was dark, and she held her hands in front of her, hoping to catch the wall before she walked into it. Without the moon, she would have no light to guide her to Thomas's quarters. She slowed. Would she make it there in the dark? She had to try.

Once her fingertips grazed the wall, she walked her hands along until she found the door handle. She tugged it open, and the hinges barely made a sound. Thank goodness for small miracles. She stretched out her hands again, intending to find the opposite wall when she tripped and fell with an *oof*, landing on a warm form below her.

A scream found its way to her throat and she clamped her lips tight as Thomas's familiar peppermint smell reached her nose.

"Ivete?" Thomas whispered. "Are you okay?"

"What are you doing *here*? I thought you'd be in your house again." She rolled off his legs, tucking her knees under her chin to lean against the cool wall.

Thomas sighed and lifted off his back to prop himself onto his elbows and look around. Ivete's eyes adjusted to the dark and his profile came into sharp relief despite the shadows.

He scrubbed his face. "I'll be in this house for the entirety of Bastien's absence, sleeping on this floor until I think Harder's men are no longer a threat."

Ivete scooted closer and placed a hand on his chest. "Are we still in danger?"

He plucked her hand from his chest and set it on the floor. "I'll be in danger if you don't find your way back to your bed."

Ivete swallowed, finding the courage to say the words she wanted to say. When she did, her words came out choppy. "You could join me."

Thomas drew a ragged breath. Ivete's heart stopped as she held her breath, waiting for his reply. He lifted to a seated position and leaned against the opposite wall, her open doorway on his left.

Ivete crawled toward him. "Kiss me again?"

Thomas placed a hand on her arm and squeezed it, preventing her approach. He closed his eyes. "Ivete, go back to bed."

She trailed her other hand along his arm, leaning closer. "Thomas." His name sounded like the plea it was.

His grip weakened. Ivete pulled from his grasp and leaned forward. With a hand on his chest, she pressed her lips to his and was met with a soft kiss. A small huff escaped Thomas's throat as he wrapped his arms around her, pulling her onto his lap and deepening the kiss.

Ivete wound her fingers into his hair and pushed closer, wanting every surface between them to touch. In the same way he'd done earlier that day, Thomas tempered his passion as if he'd shut a barn door. Stopping the kiss, he lifted her off and away from him, turning his head.

"Why are you doing this?"

Ivete's heart was still hammering from the kiss and she couldn't figure out why he had stopped her.

He spoke again into the silence. "Is this how well-off city girls treat men who work beneath them, like a plaything?"

Ivete recoiled. "What? No." How had he misunderstood? "I just want..." What did she want? Was it Thomas, or was it revenge. Was it the need to be wanted by another? To prove to herself that Henry had no need to use those club women?

"Ivete, go to bed." His voice was hard. Unyielding.

A lump formed in her throat. Ivete dipped her chin, thankful he wouldn't see how flushed she'd become. She gathered her nightgown and stood, heading for bed. Ivete shut the door with more force than necessary, realizing too late that it would wake the baby.

When the squall came, Ivete fell back on the bed and stared at the ceiling. *Poor Della*. While she was guilty of waking the child, she was more worried about the cries that could tear from her chest at any moment.

Ivete turned her face into the pillow, tears falling to be absorbed by the thick material. Was she in fact to blame for Henry's wanderings? She'd been trying to gain Thomas's affection for almost the entirety of her stay at Aster Ridge, yet his disinterest continued. Was she so undesirable? Their kiss earlier must have been simply a ruse, and the passion she thought existed only for show. A list of her many short-comings lulled her to sleep.

IVETE SLATHERED jam on two thick slices of bread. "I'm going to take breakfast to Thomas. Apparently that's something Eloise usually does."

Her mother pursed her lips. "I don't like you serving him. It's one thing to serve yourself and your family. But serving the help is another matter."

"He's not the help, Mother. He's Bastien's partner."

Della lent her support. "He is, Maxine. And he's doing much more work without Bastien here, as well as sleeping on the floor to guard us while we sleep. He needs whatever sustenance we can give him."

The tall grasses that led to the stable were wet with morning dew. Ivete cringed as she thought of the work it would take to clean her skirts. She hoped Eloise would be back in time to help. She heard Thomas in the stable. She drew a breath and let it out, trying to release the shame that clung to her. Instead, she lifted her chin and entered the office. "Good morning, Mr. McMullin. I've brought your breakfast."

Thomas's hair stuck straight up and his face looked pale and drawn. "Ivete ... about last night."

Her chest filled with dread, but she shook it off, smoothing her features so nothing showed on the outside. She walked forward and set the wrapped sandwich on the desk. When she turned to go, Thomas caught her wrist.

Ivete cut a sharp glance at his hand. His touch singed her skin all the way to her toes. He looked from her eyes to where his fingers touched her and dropped her wrist as though the heat that filled her had burned him.

He ran a hand through his hair. "I'm sorry for last night. I should not have ... done that."

Ivete lowered her brows. "You did hardly anything." She rubbed her wrist before crossing her arms. Every part of her was splayed open and more vulnerable than she ever remembered. It was as if with one touch, he leaped the social boundaries that separated them and made her believe once again that she mattered to him.

"I did far more than I should have. Bastien would have my head if he knew."

"Is that why you hold back from me?" Ivete cocked her head, hoping for an explanation to soothe her hurt pride.

"Of course. You can't think I didn't want ..." He worked his jaw, as if trying to find the right words. He cleared his throat. "I'm shocked at your interest in *me*."

She was glad he'd spent so much time searching for the right thing to say because it was perfect. He wanted her, but how could he not know his own value? How could he not see himself as she saw him? She crossed her arms over her chest and slanted him a grin, hoping to tease him into a smile. "Are you?" Ivete teased. "Does not every girl want a handsome cowboy?" She thought of the novels she read, which ended with a ride into the desert sunset.

"Cowboys don't have the funds to bring happiness to a woman like you."

Ivete frowned and took a step backward. "You've obviously been thinking about this." She studied his forlorn face. That worry had been there for more than a few hours. Thomas had considered this before last night.

He'd spent who knew how many days and weeks thinking of how unattainable she was, and she'd been thinking only of seducing him like a pawn in her game of life. Guilt and shame weighed on her heart. Same as Henry hadn't considered Ivete in his actions, Ivete had disregarded Thomas's feelings. She was no better than her fiancé, and that truth curdled in her belly.

Afraid to say or hear anything more, Ivete turned and bolted for the main house. She hit a warm body as she threw open the door. "Oof!"

Della steadied herself and smiled. "Something on fire?"

"Oh, no. I'm just …"

"Come help me, will you? These diaper cloths won't hang themselves out to dry."

"Yes, of course." Ivete followed Della to the clothes line. "Will you need much help around the place today?" She needed to work her body hard, to keep her mind occupied. Otherwise, she'd stew on Thomas and her own guilty conscience all day long.

"If you don't mind, I'd appreciate some help today."

They were side-by-side, hanging clean diaper cloths on a

line when Della spoke, breaking into her reverie. "What has you so thoughtful today?"

Ivete glanced at Della, unsure if she should tell. But before she could fully make a decision, the words tumbled out of her. "I think I might be in love with Thomas."

Della's arms, which were adjusting the clips on the line, dropped to her sides. She gaped at Ivete.

Heavens above, she should have stopped herself from saying what she'd said, truth though it may be. She closed her eyes, not ready yet to hear what Della thought.

"Love?" Della's voice was incredulous.

Ivete risked opening one eye. "I don't know. You're one of the only people I've ever met who truly loves someone."

A flicker of darkness crossed Della's face. "Start at the beginning." Della led her to a nearby bench nestled against the house.

"You know he saved me on the train. I didn't tell Bastien, but part of that was because he told the man that I was his wife. He had to kiss me to make his lie believable." Ivete noted the shock in Della's face was mixed with a bit of amusement. "Then when we realized we'd be here together, well, things were a bit awkward.

"I can imagine." Della smiled.

"But once I was here, he became my friend. He helped me with my rides, and you should have seen him during Violet's birth. He drew something out of me that I never knew I had. Shook the shock from me and spurred me into action. It was like he lent me some of his strength."

Della placed her hand on Ivete's. "You are stronger than you think. Stronger than your family thinks."

Della's words washed over her, and as it did she saw the truth in her sister's words. She squeezed Della's hands.

"Thank you." She spoke with misty eyes before she shook off the emotion and continued her story. "Well, that's why he told Harder I was his intended. I think we wouldn't have been able to pull off the married ruse, not unless we shared a room, and Thomas would never have agreed to that." Her eyes flashed with anger, but Ivete closed them, doing her best to calm herself. "He kissed me yesterday, as part of that ruse, but it wasn't acting. Della, he feels something for me. I know it."

"I don't doubt it, but what about Henry?"

"I don't know," Ivete wailed. "Mother thinks I should marry him, but I see you and Bastien, and I know there is something better out there."

"Better, but not Thomas?"

Ivete drew her brows together, waiting for Della to explain.

"I mean, if you loved Thomas, you would not be thinking of other men, other options."

Her words cut deep. Ivete knew how shallow she'd been, agreeing to marry Henry because of his money and reputation, or what it would be like to be Mrs. Burnham. But to hear it said out loud ... Ivete folded her hands on her lap to keep from clutching at her aching heart. Thomas was right. He didn't have enough money for someone as superficial as herself. She met Della's eyes, certain misery showed on her face. "I cannot work like you do, like Eloise does. You're right. Eloise is better suited to him." The words, true thought they were, tasted like poison on her tongue. She still loathed the idea of him smiling at Eloise, sliding an arm around her waist and pulling her in as Bastien so often did to Della.

"Maybe. But he has said he doesn't fancy Eloise."

"Only because I've practically been throwing myself at

him. I'm sure once I'm gone, he will see that she is a better fit for him." The idea twisted in her gut.

Della quirked a brow. "You've been throwing yourself at him?"

Ivete cursed her quick tongue, saying more than she'd intended. "I just ..." She blew through her lips. "I thought I could have a dalliance of my own, same as Henry."

"Ivete." Della's voice cut sharp. "You *wouldn't*."

"I would. Why not? Only Thomas wasn't inclined. I guess I now see why Henry did what he did. Men may flirt and tease, but I'm not the type of woman they want to bed."

Della rolled her eyes. "Nonsense." A laugh bubbled out of her. "You've asked Thomas to bed you? And he said no?" She laughed in earnest then. "I'm sorry, this is all just so preposterous. What did he say?"

Ivete couldn't help but smile, though the laughter was at her expense. "I didn't ask him in so many words, though only because I lack the courage, not because I doubted my intention."

Ivete was too ashamed to go through the horrid details of his rejection. Instead, she said, "He seems to think Bastien would kill him if he went any farther than a kiss."

"Bastien will not like even that. Not without Thomas making his intentions clear. Yours, I might add, are none too honest. Does he know you want to use him to get back at your fiancé?"

Ivete spluttered, but no sound argument came to her lips. Della was correct. "That's how it started, but now I know his feelings, I could not do that to him. On the journey to Aster Ridge he gave me reason to hope he was just as misguided as Henry and would love a dalliance of his own."

"Perhaps, but not with his friend's sister. Men have been shot for less."

Ivete threw her hands in the air. "I don't understand why Bastien cares. Henry can hurt me with his affairs, yet I cannot create joy for myself? Why do men care about the wrong things?"

Della dipped her head. "It is not your happiness that Bastien would wish to prevent, but your honor. It's not fair, I know, but too much scandal and your marriage prospects would diminish. What if you got pregnant? Your options would be quite limited, as you can imagine. Men can dally without consequence. For women, it is not so simple."

"It is not equal."

"No, it is not. Men hold power, and they must have the discipline not to wield it in the wrong way."

Ivete rolled her eyes. "Thomas is disciplined, that is certain."

"Thomas is a good man, and you should take a look at what you are doing to him. You've watched your father, your brothers, and even Henry treat women with terrible indifference. Part of you might truly believe it is acceptable. But don't forget the pain it caused in you. No matter that it is done by people who you love and respect, it isn't right. You kicking the hurt down the path isn't going to make you feel any better about what Henry did. You treating another with indifference won't make you and Henry level again. It will only rob the goodness I know you have. I see it when you interact with Bastien, with me. I see it in your patience with your mother and the way you talk to the horses. Don't lose who you are just so you can marry Henry with a proud heart."

Della's words beat a steady rhythm in Ivete's chest. The truth pressing into her limbs with every pulse.

Her mother walked into the yard with a crying Violet in her arms. "I think she is hungry." She walked to Della and passed the baby to its mother. "And what are you ladies doing out here, taking a break?"

Ivete stood, giving Della a meaningful gaze. "I'm going to strip the bed in the guesthouse."

Better to have the guest house ready for Thomas to move back in. No doubt Ivete would wake with some hair brained idea and make a fool of herself once more. The further he was from her. The better.

17

Ivete entered the guesthouse and inhaled the scent of Thomas. The cool aroma of the peppermints he kept in his pocket for the horses. A smile played on her lips as she thought of their kiss. A thump came from one of the back rooms.

"Thomas?" she called out. Though she'd been here a month already, she hadn't ever explored the guest house and wandered in the direction she thought the bedroom lay. She smiled to think of Thomas throwing out his fears of Harder's return and moving back in here before Bastien's return. He must be willing to take the risk if it meant he could be farther away from Ivete's wanton ways. As she made her way to the back, Thomas didn't reply, and she heard no more noise. "Thomas, are you teasing me?" She hoped he was. Wanton or not, she hoped she could ask him for another kiss like the one he'd given her last night. She pushed open the bedroom door and gasped when she found the bedroom in total disarray. Tables were turned over. The quilts were a rumpled mess on the floor. A crock was shattered on the ground.

The door behind her slammed and she jumped at the noise.

Arms grabbed her from behind, and hand pressed over her mouth. "Don't scream." The voice was gravelly and unfamiliar.

Ivete tried to break free of the stranger's grip. Was it Aaron? Had he returned to hurt Thomas?

The man squeezed her tighter. She couldn't breathe. If he applied any more pressure, she'd be killed like a mouse in a python's grip. She relaxed in his hands.

His breath was hot on her ears. "Good girl."

He threw her onto the disheveled bed and pointed a pistol at her face. "Don't scream."

Ivete gulped through her dry throat and nodded her assent. She didn't recognize the man, only knew he wasn't Harder.

The man's gaze pierced her as dangerously as the barrel of the gun. "Is Harder coming back?"

She shook her head.

"Did he leave anything here?"

Ivete looked around the room. It was impossible to tell if there was anything that didn't belong.

"I don't know." Her voice was small and she hated herself for the fear that came through.

"Maybe your man will know." He flicked the pistol in a motion that commanded her to stand. "Let's go ask."

Ivete stood, but was afraid to move closer to the filthy bandit. With one step, the man took her by her hair and shoved her toward the back entrance. As she pulled the door open, he clasped her arm in a painful grip. He drew near so his lips brushed her ear. "Don't try anything." Before he drew away, he took a long sniff of her hair. Ivete closed her eyes at the molestation. He tugged her toward the back of the barn. As they traversed the space between buildings, Ivete's eyes searched the landscape for Della or her mother. Maxine could use a rifle as well as Ivete, and Della would be able to get away with Violet. The thought of her niece being in danger pinched her heart. She whimpered.

Once they were in the shade of the barn, the man's voice boomed through the stables. "Thomas!"

The horses that were inside nickered at the shout. Ivete scanned the space, torn between hoping he would come to her aid and hoping he was far away from this evil man.

Her captor gripped her arm. "Where is he?"

Ivete shook her head, unable to find words.

Thomas's voice, then his silhouette, came from a stall at the front of the stable. "Rogers. What are you doing back here?"

"Just looking for my old friend. Where did he go?"

"Harder left last night." Thomas clenched a rag in his hands so tightly his knuckles glowed white.

"And his gold?"

"Took it with him, I suppose."

Rogers yanked Ivete, crashing her into his chest. He locked his arm around her neck, clicked the hammer on his pistol, and touched the cold metal to her temple.

Thomas stretched his hands out. "Rogers, I don't know what you're looking for. Harder is gone and he didn't leave anything here."

"He didn't have it with him. I watched him go."

"It must be in the guest house."

Rogers shook his head and his beard brushed Ivete's hair. "I already looked. All I found was this one." He twisted the cold barrel of the gun against her head.

"I promise you. I have nothing. That woman you hold is

dear to me and I would not risk her life for any amount of gold."

A horse stepped out of the stall behind Thomas. It was saddled and apparently curious as to why the ride hadn't started. It ducked its head and lipped at Thomas's pocket. He brushed the animal's nose and stepped away.

"I ain't leavin' here empty handed. You give me the gold or I take her with me." The barrel of the pistol pressed into her flesh, crushing it against her skull. She grimaced, closing her eyes in search of the courage she found the night of Violet's birth. She recalled Thomas's ability to pull that bravery from inside her. She opened her eyes and searched his, hoping to locate that strength, but fear shone back as he watched Rogers. With the gun against her temple, she had no chance of getting away. The best she could do would be to remove herself from this position.

Thomas's words broke into her planning. "Take the mares. Take as many as you want."

Ivete's heart leapt with joy at the suggestion, but her voice sounded as though it possessed a mind of its own. "You can't give away the horses. Your ranch."

Thomas held Ivete's gaze for a moment, then hardened as they switched to Rogers's again. "I'll help you saddle and tie them together."

Ivete couldn't see Rogers's face, but his hold loosened slightly, and she thought he might be considering it. Then it tightened once more. "Not enough. You have more."

Thomas's face fell. "I don't. I only work here, and the man who owns this ranch will be gone for another week yet."

Rogers backed away from Thomas, taking Ivete with him. "Then we'll see you in one week."

"Thomas!" Ivete cried, afraid if she lost sight of him now,

she might never see him again. She struggled against the man, no longer caring whether he shot her. Wherever he would take her, she was certain it would be a fate worse than death.

Thomas reached under his vest for the pistol he kept holstered. He pointed it in their direction. If he took the shot he may very well hit her and not his true mark, but she trusted Thomas with her life. She stilled and closed her eyes, praying Thomas was as good at aiming as he was at soothing horses.

The thunderous bang came. Rogers's hold broke. Ivete slumped to the floor, her legs numb and useless. An unknown part of Rogers anatomy brushed her back and she scrambled away through the loose hay on the ground.

Thomas strode toward her, his gun trained on Rogers, his voice as gritty as any cowboy's ever was. "Leave, or I'll put the next one between your eyes."

Ivete froze, afraid to check how close Rogers was, afraid to hear whether he would call Thomas's bluff. Instead, she watched Thomas.

His eyes lifted, as though he was following Rogers's retreating form, then his attention fell to Ivete. He reached out a hand. "Are you hurt?"

She shook her head and reached out to him. He tugged her to her feet and placed both hands on the sides of her face. He raked his gaze over her frame. When he deemed her safe enough, he crushed her to him, one hand wrapped around her waist and the other knitted into her hair. Ivete held him, too, fear drenching her face in tears and wracking her body with sobs.

Thomas released her and took her by the shoulders. "What is it?"

A hysterical giggle bubbled from her mouth. "I don't

know. I'm safe now, only ..." She held her arm aloft and watched her trembling hand.

"We aren't safe yet. I need to check on Della and your mother."

Ivete's breath caught in her throat. How could she have forgotten about them? She rushed out of the barn, the daylight blinding compared to the darkness within the barn and in the man who had held her captive only moments ago.

Thomas caught up with ease, going through the entry first, his voice filling the home. "Della? Maxine?"

A shocked Della came around the corner, drying her hands on a towel.

Thomas rushed toward her. "Are you hurt? Where are Violet and Maxine."

Della's confusion was plain on her face as she spoke. "Violet is napping in the cot and Maxine is ..."

Ivete's mother came into view. "I'm here. What is all this shouting about? You could have woken the babe. Was that a gunshot I heard?"

Thomas strode past the women and down the hall to Della and Bastien's room, Ivete close on his heels. Violet lay sleeping in her cot in Bastien and Della's bedroom.

Ivete collapsed against the wall, releasing a sigh. She took Thomas's hand in both of hers. "They're all safe."

He pulled her into his arms once again and set his chin on her hair. "They're all safe."

Ivete relaxed into his arms, letting his thumping heartbeat soothe her racing heart.

Della's whisper came from the doorway. "What is this all about?"

Thomas and Ivete broke apart. They made their way out of the bedroom and down the hall before Thomas spoke.

"Harder's man returned. He thought Harder left gold here and he wanted to take it, or Ivete, with him."

Della's eyes widened. "He's here?" Her eyes flashed to Ivete. "He wanted you?"

Ivete's emotions still pulsed beyond her control. She tugged Della in for an embrace. Waving her mother into it, too. She wrapped one arm around her mother and held two of the three women who were most dear to her.

Thomas's voice came from the side. "He's off the property by now, without one of his ears."

Ivete released her mama and Della and turned to Thomas. "You shot his ear?"

He nodded.

Ivete waved her finger at him. "Careful, your pride is showing."

Maxine spoke in the proper voice she used with guests back in Chicago. "I, for one, have had enough Wild West adventures. The lawlessness out here is too much. I'll send a letter to your father as soon as I'm able." She turned to Della. "Are you sure you and Bastien wouldn't be safer and more comfortable in Chicago? Francis gifted Luc and Angelica a home. I'm certain he would do the same for you and Bastien."

Della smiled. "I appreciate the offer. It has been quite an adventure for you two, but it is not usually so dramatic. In fact, without you two here, it can sometimes even be boring." Disbelief clung to her last words.

Ivete laughed, and a sliver of the tension in her chest eased.

Thomas's shoulders seemed to relax, too. "Well, no damage done in the long run, but we certainly got a good scare." His gaze scanned Ivete, as though checking once more that she was fine.

Ivete's hand flew to her mouth. "Oh! But there was damage. To your bedroom. Come see." She fled from the house, Thomas hot on her heels.

"I can inspect the damage on my own, Ivete," he called.

But she didn't stop. She needed to run, to release the energy coursing through. She stopped once she stood within Thomas's shattered, disarranged room.

Thomas groaned and stepped forward, setting an overturned table upright. Ivete joined him and they worked in companionable silence for a bit.

Thomas cleared his throat. "How did you know about my ranch?" His voice was soft as he plucked the broken crockery from the floor.

"Bastien told me. I hope you don't mind."

"Not at all. I would have told you myself if it had come into conversation."

"Where are your siblings now?"

"Scattered mostly. Last I heard, my youngest sister was living with the Harders."

Ivete stopped, fear for his sister ballooning in her chest.

Her alarm must have shown because Thomas laughed. "The Harders are good people. It's only Aaron who leads a life of danger. Katherine Harder was like a mother to me, especially when my father remarried."

Ivete nodded. She tried to associate the name Harder with good, but it only brought fear. "All the more reason to not give up the broodmares. You need to get your ranch started. Soon."

Thomas stopped, his gaze penetrating. "Nothing would have forced me to allow him to take you away."

His stare stole her breath. "I'll just ..." Ivete pulled a bundle of sheets into her arms and made for the door. Once out of his sight she found she could breathe normally once more. What had come over her? Why was she so shaken that he would protect her so fiercely? After all, Bastien had left her in his care. Of course he would do whatever it took to save someone he was responsible for. He would not risk harming his partnership with Bastien. And on the train? Thomas must have some compulsive need to rescue damsels. He really was like the cowboys in her novels. But Ivete was no girl who needed saving. No, Ivete was the villain. Selfish and shallow. She caused grief to all who surrounded her.

18

As he tended the stock, Thomas thought of how Ivete had run away from him twice now, both times when he'd shared a sliver of what he felt for her. He tried to think what he'd said wrong.

Thomas was almost grateful for the dead cow when he found it a few hours later. It gave him something to do other than obsess over Ivete. He sliced the earth with the shovel, pushed, and tossed another load of dirt to the side. He tried to imagine each toss was a thought he was getting rid of, but it did no good. His confusion returned every time. Why had she seemed so surprised by his dedication to her? How could she have thought he would allow Rogers to take her away? Or that he kissed women without feeling? If she did believe him a rogue, what was she doing coming to him in the night?

He plunged the shovel into the rich soil. The effort reminded him of the years planting with his family. Diseased cows were a blight of their own. Instead of causing the crops to bend and die, it took the beasts from healthy to buried in a single day. As a child, his family experienced difficult seasons in farming. He tried to encourage himself that these years came, and they went. But with every shovelful of earth, he thought of the wasted money he was burying and how much further he was from a ranch of his own.

Harder's talk of ranching together, though it may never happen, ignited that original zeal to start on his own. Without a wife, he could live in a tent if necessary. He could do anything to get himself started. He regretted accepting Bastien's offer. Though it had been generous at the time, it was becoming less so with each dead cow.

He drew a mental map of Montana and thought about where he would like to settle. Dragonfly Creek was a beautiful spot and near enough to his siblings that any of them could make their way there. If he stayed nearby, he and Bastien could continue their partnership and crossbreed their horses, a cost-saving benefit to both.

It didn't matter where he landed, only that he not waste any more time building the business of others, no matter the pay.

The words he'd spoken to Ivete were true. A woman like her could never be happy with a man with as little means as he. Then why did it pain him so to watch her run? Though his mind understood reason and logic, his heart held only regret, for the truth and for having to speak those facts to Ivete. She was no fool. She must have already known this, yet she still invited him to her bed. His mind spun with questions, and he wondered when, or if, he would get the chance to ask them.

Moments later, he found Ivete in the stable, brushing down a horse. She wore his hat, the one he kept on the wall of the office for Sundays. His heart lifted at the sight. "You shouldn't be out here alone, Ivete." His voice was hard, and he took a calming breath hoping to rein in the emotions that rocked him.

"You've been out for a bit." Her voice was guarded.

Thomas took shallow breaths. "Lost another cow. We need to get them to the market while we still have some left."

"How many have died?"

"Today makes five. A quarter of the herd."

"When do you expect Bastien home?"

Thomas shook his head. "No idea. I'm not going to rush him either. The loss of a friend ... I can't imagine."

Ivete gave a somber nod, her mouth turned down. "No riders today. Mother has been keeping a dutiful eye on the horizon." Ivete threw him a look. "As long as Mama watches the window, she doesn't have to do anything more... strenuous." She placed the brush in the bucket and dusted off her hands. He noticed her dress wasn't fancy like the ones she'd worn at the start of her stay. Instead she wore a casual skirt and a shirt and vest on top. This new attire and his hat made her look like a regular frontier woman.

He smiled at the thought. "That's good. You know, Harder told me he was done with thieving. Said goodbye to the gang and is off on his own."

"Do you believe him?"

"Must be, if Rogers came back. He wouldn't have done that if Harder was leading them. I don't doubt he would have killed Aaron for that gold he came for." Thomas heaved a sigh. "I hope he's done." He glanced at Ivete. He longed to go to her, to take her into his arms and tell her just what other things he hoped. But after she'd come to him in the night, he feared any encouragement on his part might lead to ruin on hers.

He crossed his arms and considered how she'd changed

these last weeks. She met his gaze and he noticed hers held none of the demureness she'd shown on the train. She was comfortable with him now, enough to show her true self and not whatever society thought appropriate. "You're happy here." It wasn't a question. What he wasn't certain of, was if she was equally happy in Chicago. She hardly spoke of the city. Was the omission intentional?

Ivete stepped closer and lifted a hand to his cheek. He kept his arms crossed, a necessary barrier against this woman who took what she wanted. A look of sadness crossed her features, and she lifted onto her toes to plant a kiss on his lips. It wasn't a kiss to satisfy a need, not like the one she'd given him that night. This one was soft, almost a question.

Maxine's voice called from outside. "Ivete!"

Rather than flinch away, Ivete took her time drawing from him, and with a somber nod, she left.

Thomas had barely taken a full breath when she returned. "Thomas. Riders." Her voice quivered.

He jogged toward Ivete and looked outside. Several riders made their way toward them along the road. Thomas wrapped an arm around her. "To the house. Have the rifle ready."

Thomas swung onto the bareback of the horse Ivete had been brushing down and rode out to meet the strangers. They were too well-dressed to be Harder's men.

Thomas tipped his hat at the gentlemen. "Afternoon."

"Is this Aster Ridge Ranch?" The oldest man spoke. He was flanked by two younger men.

"That's us. What can I do you for?"

"Francis Graham. Pleased to meet you. I believe Bastien is expecting us. This is my son Willem and my future son-in-law Henry."

"Ivete's future husband?" Thomas asked, though his spirit folded in on itself, crushing and pressing smaller, tighter inside him. He knew the answer before the man confirmed it. Hadn't Ivete told him the wedding was off? Thomas's mind sifted through the memories trying to sort out where that idea had come from. Only words weren't everything. Hadn't she *shown* him she wasn't engaged? And yet...

Thomas eyed both men and had to tear his gaze away from Henry. He reined his horse around and rode next to Francis. "I'm sorry to tell you that Bastien has gone to attend the death of a friend. We don't expect him back for another week more."

"That is no concern. I'll be glad to put my feet up and see my wife and daughter."

Thomas pulled his heart deeper into his chest. "They'll be mighty glad to see you. We've not felt safe without Bastien here."

The brother, Willem, spoke from behind. "Truly? I never thought of Bastien as the bodyguard type."

Thomas turned in his saddle. "Maybe not, but I'll be glad for any man who can hold a rifle. I was on the train that was robbed, and they stole three of our broodmares. The leader of that gang thought to return them and has only just left."

"Blast," Willem continued. "I would have dearly liked to meet the fellow. Is he the one in all the Wanted posters? Aaron Harder?"

Thomas resented Willem's thrill at such a serious topic. "Yes."

Willem hammered the horn on his saddle. "What did I tell you, Henry? We're bound to have an adventure or two." He turned to Thomas again. "When I heard of the train robbery, I told my father I wanted to come along to fetch the women. It's no wonder the west has so hypnotized Bastien. Adventure and a pretty wife." He whistled with glee.

Henry nodded. "A pretty woman does a lot for a place." He grinned, an oily, smug expression Thomas wanted to strike from his face.

When they were almost to the house, Maxine exited, followed by Ivete and Della.

"Francis!" Maxine cried, "Oh, am I ever so glad to see you." She walked up to her husband's mount. "We thought you might be more bandits, come to take us away."

Henry's voice rang out from behind. "Not likely *she'd* be in any such danger."

Ivete jerked from behind Maxine and stopped as though she'd been hit by lightning. The movement, or lack of it, caught Thomas's attention, and he watched as she gaped at Henry.

"Darling," Henry drawled, urging his mount around Thomas and sliding off to pull Ivete into his arms.

She stiffened at Henry's touch and stood rigid in his embrace, her gaze trained on Thomas all the while. Ivete's eyes showed a silent plea, but Thomas jerked his chin away only to meet Willem's curious stare.

Thomas's pride swelled. He kicked his horse forward and rode into the barn without a glance behind him. Let the men take care of their horses. He wasn't a servant. Their fancy clothes meant nothing out here. The clop of Willem's horse's hooves alerted Thomas to his approach.

"This is a fine stable. Is it filled?" Willem asked.

"Not quite. We hope it will be by next spring."

"We should have bought better mounts in Billings. These are fine, but nothing like the one you are riding."

Willem eyed the Roan mare that Harder had recently returned.

"She's a beauty," Thomas agreed.

"Well, I'm here to help. I want to see what it is like being a cowboy." He rubbed his hands together and glanced around the stable, dimly lit from the evening sun.

"Chores are done for the day. We just need to stable these, and soon the ladies will have supper ready."

Willem slapped a hand to his belly. "I could use a giant meal. Riding all day took it out of me."

The two men worked in companionable silence. Thomas led Willem to a stall for his horse.

"That one is a beaut, too." He pointed to Midnight.

"Careful," Thomas warned. "She's been a might restless. She'll be birthing tonight or tomorrow."

"You don't say?" Willem's face shone. "Can I help?"

Thomas laughed. "If you want. It's a messy business."

"I can handle the mess. I'm here to get the full experience. I already missed being robbed. I won't miss the birth of Bastien's stock."

Thomas put his horse in her stall and started for Midnight's. "Gettin' close, girl?" He reached for her, but Midnight tossed her head. He leaned to the side to check if her teats had dropped but couldn't see with the fading daylight. There wasn't any sweat on her neck, so he waved Willem toward the exit to find their supper. When they neared the house, they found Henry and Francis's horses tied to the rail.

Thomas cast a look at Willem, his brows raised.

The other man grinned. "I'll help you, mate."

They each took a horse and repeated the process from before.

Willem chuckled. "Better keep Henry's mount away

from your mares. No sense birthing one of *his* offspring. The man doesn't know much about horses, and his choice of horseflesh shows it. Only don't attempt to go toe-to-toe with him in banking."

"I'll keep that in mind." Thomas could think of one thing he'd like to go toe-to-toe about, but he doubted Ivete would choose him anyhow. He recalled the shock on Ivete's face when she'd seen Henry, and she had said the wedding had been called off. Yet ... if Francis was calling Henry her fiancé, there had to be some discrepancy between her claims and reality.

When Willem and Thomas entered the house, they found Della and Ivete in the kitchen while Maxine entertained Francis and Henry near the unlit fireplace. Each man had a glass of alcohol in their hands.

Willem leaned in. "Apparently, Chicago propriety doesn't apply here. I wouldn't mind a glass myself."

Ivete pulled her brother in for a hug. "Willem, I didn't know you were coming. Rather, I didn't realize *any* of you were on your way so soon."

"Did Father not tell you? He thought to stay a few weeks and bring you ladies back in time for Thanksgiving."

Ivete's eyes flashed to Thomas. He jerked his gaze away and stepped into the kitchen to help Della. "What can I do?"

"Oh, Thomas, you don't need to help me. No doubt you're dead on your feet."

"Nonsense. You've just gained three guests, all of whom I hear are famished."

Della flashed him a smile. "You're a gem. Can you check the biscuits in the oven? If they're golden on top, take them out."

Thomas set to work. Soon, Ivete slipped into the crowded kitchen, bumping into Thomas in the tight space.

She took his wrist and looked at him with wide eyes. Only her courage must have failed her because her eyes darted to the room where the three men who represented her real-life sat in leisure while Della worked to frantically make enough food for the additions.

She squeezed his hand. "I didn't know they were coming." Her voice was low enough that Della might not hear.

Thomas studied her eyes and the set of her mouth. "Your father seems to think he is gaining a son-in-law very soon." He pulled himself free of her grip and found a pot to fill. Della hadn't asked for one, but it didn't matter. He stormed outside to the pump and furiously worked the handle. Too soon, the pot was overflowing, and he straightened, not yet ready to face Ivete.

All this time, she'd been engaged, yet she'd led him to believe she had feelings for him. He shook his head at the foolish games of women. He recalled his childhood with Aaron. The Harder family had been poor from the start. Aaron's father drank their money away, while his mother had nearly as many children as Thomas's family. Though poor as dirt, Aaron was handsome, and the girls didn't care where he came from. Their families, on the other hand, cared very much. The girls would tug Aaron around for months until a father or brother arrived to show him his place. This was one of the reasons he and Aaron set off on their own. Start afresh with none of the bias of a small town.

Yet somehow, Thomas had found a woman whose family would chase him off if they understood his intentions. He was a fool not to choose a girl like Eloise, whose family might appreciate a match between Thomas and one of their daughters. He thought of the way Mrs. Morris had thanked him for delivering Eloise the night of Harder's arrival. How she'd fawned over him and been sure to remark on Eloise's beauty and her need for a strong man.

Thomas picked up the pot and readied himself to go back inside the house.

Ivete exited as the screen door slapped back into place. Without a single look at him, she marched to the henhouse. Setting the pot near the house, Thomas followed.

"Thomas!" She pressed her hand to her heart as though he'd startled her. She rushed to explain. "Della wanted eggs, said she could make a custard if we had enough."

He grasped her wrist as she had taken his in the kitchen and held her gaze, daring her to look away.

She didn't.

He took one deep breath. "Are you marrying him?" The question was another dare, and he wasn't entirely sure he wanted her to rise to the challenge. One little yes from her lips might burn his heart to cinders.

19

Thomas held onto her, but he didn't need to. His question pinned her in place as thoroughly as any tether. "I ... I don't know."

The question didn't have a simple answer. Technically she was engaged. She'd promised her mother she wouldn't convey any decisions to Henry until she'd taken some space in Montana. Henry wasn't supposed to come fetch her like this.

Thomas stepped closer, fire in his eyes, but there was a plea there too. "What do you mean? Are you two engaged, or not?"

"I'm engaged, but I don't want to marry him. I wanted to break things before we came out, but my mother made me promise to wait." These words were no heavenly inspiration. She'd known this from the moment that woman had approached her in the street. But speaking them to Thomas was different than telling herself or her mother. Thomas was the only other person who might be equally affected by her decision. "I don't love him. He had ... relations with another woman before Mother and I left for Aster Ridge. I left a scandal behind, and that is likely what I will return to."

"So in your escape from scandal you try to stir one up out here, with me? Are you sure it was him and not you that caused the gossip?"

His words hurt, so close to what she feared— that Henry's infidelity was her fault, that everyone thought her a fool for her reaction. Her chest ached with the wound to her heart. Pained as she was, she wanted Thomas to understand. His face was so stern, so unforgiving.

"I never wrote to him. I never dreamed he would come here."

"Not writing to your fiancé is a far cry from jumping on me in the night. You invited me to your bed, yet you loved another."

"I didn't jump on you, I fell. And I don't love him!" His accusation and refusal to listen to her hardened her resolve and she glared at him.

He met her glare with one of his own. "Why did you invite me to your bed?" His voice was flat.

She tossed her head as her cheeks heated. "You shouldn't speak of it."

"Ivete," he growled.

"I wanted it. I wanted you. Is that what you want to hear?"

"No, I hoped to hear much more than that. You didn't want me, you wanted to please yourself. To prove heaven knows what to your fiancé. I'll not be a player in this game." He spat the words as though they were bitter in his mouth and turned to go.

"Thomas, wait!" she cried, tripping in her haste to reach him. He turned with a gentle hand to help her up again. "I was wrong to treat you that way. But you're not a piece in any game. You mean more to me."

"You're a fisherwoman. You know you can't have two fish on the same line." He shook his head. "You didn't tell me you were engaged."

"I thought you knew!" Ivete threw her hands in the air. "My mother won't seem to *stop* talking about Henry."

Thomas held her gaze as he shook his head. "I didn't know."

As soon as he spoke the words, Ivete knew them to be true. Knew he'd lost a bit of his honor with her deception.

"I'm sorry." The apology wasn't enough and she knew it. "I treated you badly. I acted like..." Henry. Ivete swallowed, desperation clawing at her throat as she stopped the excuses. She knew too much to get away with what she'd done. Knew that while she might have been a product of her upbringing, that environment didn't exist at Aster Ridge. She'd been a fool to pretend that Thomas was like Henry and that he would accept her treatment of him. "My reasons may have been flawed, but my feelings were real."

Thomas blinked at her. She wished he would come to her, provide comfort like he'd done when news of Simon's death had reached them. Her body ached with a similar helplessness.

Thomas cleared his throat. "Sort things out with Henry. Until then, I need you to let me alone."

He turned once more, but this time Ivete was out of fire. She didn't have the desire to chase him down like before. What else could she say? He was right. She had no business trying to soothe his hurt until she cleared away any questions regarding Henry.

Ivete gripped the side of the chicken coop as she watched him walk away. She felt like a cutthroat trout from the lake, sliced and gutted before being brought inside for dinner.

Tears blurred her vision as she searched for eggs. When she returned to the house, Thomas wasn't inside.

"Where is Thomas?" Ivete asked Della.

Della shook her head, "I don't know. Food is ready though. If he's hungry, he'll be in soon enough." She looked at Ivete for the first time since her return. "No eggs ... What's wrong?"

Ivete's lip trembled, and she swallowed the cry threatening to rise. "He is angry with me."

Della's shoulders lifted with a sigh. "The time for deciding has come and gone. None of the people in that room are going to have much patience with your indecision."

Stepping away, Della clapped her hands and called, "Supper is ready."

While everyone found their seats, Ivete helped to put the food on the table.

Henry sidled close, putting a hand around her waist and whispering in her ear. "This country air suits you, my darling."

Such a gesture back in Chicago would have made Ivete giddy. Now it only served to make her cringe. He released his hold and took his seat next to her. With Bastien gone, the seating was shuffled, and Ivete found herself on the end without a partner across from her.

Henry turned to his host. "This meal looks wonderful. You are a wonder with your ability to run a household."

Ivete glanced at her mother, who was staring with lowered brows. Ivete mouthed, *what?* Her mother gave a slow shake of her head. Ivete knew her mother well enough to know the woman wouldn't appreciate a scene and Ivete was to behave like the lady she'd been taught. Ivete wiped the emotion from her face and plastered on a smile.

Willem looked around the room. "Where is Thomas? I came to think he might join us for supper. I have loads of questions for him."

Della answered. "I suppose he has found himself a task. He knows better than to miss dinner. I'm sure he'll be in shortly."

"If I weren't so hungry, I might seek him out and join him in whatever task he has found. I find the cowboy life quite interesting. My friends are all jealous that I get to come for this visit. I daresay Bastien could start a gentlemen's club of some sort. Housing guests and letting them feel like strong men, working the land and herding the cattle. He could even charge them to do his work. What would you say to that, Father?"

Francis bobbed his head. "You might have a worthy endeavor there, though I wonder at Bastien's role. He's keen to leave us behind. Bringing the city out here might not be of interest to him."

Willem leaned forward in his seat. "What do you say, Della?"

"I think he would love a bit of free labor." She gave Willem a smirk and took a sip of her drink.

Henry leaned forward over the table. "I think it fabulous. But what can the women do? Surely you don't think men would stay for long without any women to entertain?"

Ivete's cheeks burned with his insinuation. How had she never noticed his obsession with women before. Had she truly been so blinded by his position in society? Or had she been too self-absorbed to think his every comment about a woman was referencing her and not another?

Willem spoke with his mouth full. "I think many might

come for the food alone. Della, Bastien mentioned your cooking, but surely this has been done with the help of the goddess Hestia."

Della smirked, clearly not buying her brother-in-law's sugary compliments.

Thomas entered, stopping at the ewer to grab the bar of soap and tossing it in the air and catching it. "Midnight is in labor. We might have a foal born tonight or tomorrow." He turned to leave again, and the table sat in stunned silence.

Willem clapped his hands together once and rubbed them like the villain in a book. "People would most definitely pay for this experience. Surely Thomas can time the births to happen every month."

The latch on the front door signaled Thomas's return, and Willem hitched his voice so he could hear. "Will you sleep in the barn, my man?"

Thomas took his seat next to Willem and avoided Ivete's stare. "I will. I'll be glad for some company if you mean to assist."

"Certainly. I've never birthed a horse before, or anything for that matter."

Violet wailed at that moment, causing the table to erupt in laughter. Before Della had time to stand, Maxine stood and lifted the baby from her place on the sofa. Her mother whispered into the child's ears, and the crying stopped.

Ivete watched her mother with respectful gratitude. If she loved Violet so, it made sense that she also loved each of her children as much. Ivete had always tried to be a credit to her mother, but now, seeing her with Violet, Ivete could see the real joy she might also have brought.

Henry nudged Ivete and followed her gaze to the grandmother and baby. "You'll be a great mother."

"Thank you," Ivete choked out, the words bitter on her

tongue.

"What is it? Have you eaten something bad?"

Ivete smiled. "It's nothing. The food is wonderful."

"I saw you helped your dear sister. Are you becoming much of a chef?"

Ivete laughed. "Not at all. We've been without a maid these past two days, and I must say I cannot wait for her return." Once again, her hasty words took a new meaning after they were spoken, and her eyes flashed to Thomas. He was listening to Willem, who spoke about his plans for a gentleman's ranch, but the muscles in his jaw stuck out like a button on a too-tight coat.

Once the meal was finished, the family settled at the fireplace, leaving Della and Ivete to the task of dishes. The work wasn't backbreaking, but the idea that Eloise could be here and Ivete resting by the fireplace made it painful to bear. Afraid to address Thomas directly, she pleaded her case to Della. "Surely we can get Eloise back tomorrow. There are now four men here. She is plenty safe. Willem could even escort her to and from the ranch every day." She eyed her brother, gesturing with his hands to a listening Thomas, who dodged a finger to the eye. "I daresay he'd love the idea of protecting a young woman from thieves and Indians."

Della laughed. "I'll ask Thomas. Your father and brother may be here, but Bastien left Thomas in charge. If he isn't comfortable, I will not suggest it again."

"Where is everyone going to sleep?" Ivete rolled her sleeves and scraped leftover food from a plate before dunking it in the pot of water Thomas had delivered.

"If Thomas is done sleeping on the floor, we have one bedroom open in the house, and the guest house has two more." Della lowered her voice to a whisper. "I thought

Henry should sleep away from Thomas. Maybe Willem can join Thomas in the guest house."

Once the dishes were done, Maxine joined them in the kitchen. "This one is hungry again." She bounced Violet in her arms, the child's wails faint but unending. Her big blue eyes glistened with tears.

Della took the baby and cast a glance at Ivete. "Will you let Willem and Thomas know my sleeping arrangements? I think they've made their way to the barn." She turned to Maxine. "I thought to have Henry in the extra room and Willem and Thomas out in the guest house. That way, Willem can be part of Thomas's every adventure."

Ivete smiled, but it didn't go beyond her face. Her heart was hammering away thinking of Thomas, though out of fear or longing she could not tell.

Her heart kept up its frantic beat even though she strode slowly toward the barn and slowed down even more once she was close enough to hear voices rising near Midnight's stall.

"Oh, hey, Sis." Willem glanced at her, then back to Thomas.

"You're not in there with her?" Ivete asked. Both men were leaning on the ledge of the stall, watching the laboring mare.

"Not yet. She'd only be angry with us. Actually, I'd like to get all the horses locked out of their stalls for the night. They can sleep in the pasture and give Midnight as much privacy as possible."

"Sure." Willem leapt at the opportunity, striding away to close all the outer doors to the stable.

Once he was out of ear shot Ivete spoke. "Della asked that you and Willem share the guest house, though I wonder if you'll get any sleep at all tonight."

Thomas nodded and turned back to the horse.

"I hope Willem isn't a pain. I usually can't stand him when he gets one of his foolish notions."

Thomas kept his back to her as he spoke. "The Graham children like adventure."

Ivete smiled. It would appear that way, especially compared to their parents.

Thomas's voice was gruff. "Is that what this is for you? A taste of the west before you go back to your real life?"

"N-" Ivete clamped her mouth as Willem came down the neck of the stable.

He threw an arm about Ivete's shoulders, a goofy smile on his face. "You going to join us tonight?"

"No." her voice was sharper than it ought to be. "This isn't a vacation. These foals will impact both Bastien and Thomas's livelihoods." She prayed he took her admonition as his answer. This was no adventure for her or for them. She understood that. Now.

"Easy, Sis. I'm not planning to slaughter the poor creature. Only watch as this cowboy here shows me a thing or two."

With a final glance at Thomas's back, Ivete stormed from the stables.

WHEN SHE ENTERED THE HOUSE, Henry called to her from the plush armchair where he was seated near her father. He'd done little else besides sitting on his backside since he arrived. He had no care for her, or for Della who gained a break only because Violet needed nursing. Ivete didn't doubt that, if she could, Della would have nursed standing up so she could continue her chores.

Thomas had turned his back on her and Henry proved

himself every moment more of a headache she wanted nothing to do with. Her body nearly collapsed under the weight of it all. She wrapped her arms around herself and turned toward the hallway. "I'm not feeling well. I think I'll turn in early."

"Darling?" Her mother sprang from her spot on the hearth and cupped Ivete's elbow with one hand while the other pressed against Ivete's forehead. "You don't look well. You are flushed. Let's get you into bed." She led Ivete to her room and closed the door behind them. Her mother's face was earnest as she sat on the bed next to Ivete. "Are you truly ill, or is it Henry's appearance?"

Ivete sniffed at her mother's keen assessment. "I still don't want to marry him. Can't I stay here?"

"Darling, the gossip will disappear in time. You cannot run away because your enemies latch onto your pain."

"It isn't them. I don't sleep well in the city. I have no real purpose ..." Ivete hadn't voiced these thoughts, and they were like a brick wall. Each word spoken turned her thoughts into a viable reality.

"I told you I should have allowed you more command of the household. We will start when we return. Della has given you a bit of learning, but much of what she does will be of no use to you in the city."

"It's not that I want to run a household. There is something here. I fear if I leave, I may never get it back."

"Is it to do with a certain stable boy?"

"He's not a boy, mother. He is older than I am."

"He is working for your brother, with no prospects of his own. He's not yet a man until he can provide for a family. You two have been spending too much time with one another."

"Hardly. I see him when I ride and at dinner."

189

Her mother pursed her lips but said no more.

"I'll not marry Henry. I don't know how to tell him. The nerve of him coming along with Daddy is enough to make me spit. I was not happy with him when I left. I made no pretense."

"It is a sign that he loves you, despite your outburst."

"Yes, well, I don't love him and his faults."

Her mother closed her eyes and flared her nostrils. "Ivete, you loved him not three months ago. You cannot be rash."

"I'm not rash." Ivete's voice was stern. "At your request, I didn't break the engagement before I left. I'll not keep the lie any longer."

"Your father plans to leave in two weeks. You need not lie, but you will act with the decency befitting a Graham." Although her words were harsh, her mother patted her hand before standing to go. "I hope you feel better in the morning."

The door closed, and Ivete was finally alone. The anger at her mother bled into sadness over Thomas's refusal to hear her or even look at her. She undressed, hanging the plain, sturdy clothes she'd borrowed from Della next to her finer wardrobe. She looked at the clothing hung side by side. One half held beautiful silks and satins that were unfit for Montana and must be carefully handled. The other side was plain and sturdy, meant for toil and hardship. Not even she understood why she preferred Della's drab calicos. No wonder it was impossible for her mother to fathom Ivete's preference.

SHE AWOKE at the sound of a latch and a light behind her bedroom door. She lifted her head and watched as a figure came through the door. "Th—"

"Darling, I hope I didn't frighten you." Henry's face held a gleam similar to one Willem would wear, mischievous and impulsive.

"What are you doing?"

"We haven't had a chance to speak, and I hoped to find you alone."

"Of course I am alone. Did you expect to find me with a bedmate?" Ivete scooted so her back was against the headboard and crossed her arms over her chest in an effort to hide her night dress. When she'd tripped over Thomas in the hallway her dress had not felt inappropriate, but with Henry's leer tracing every inch of her, she desperately wanted more layers between them.

"I spoke with Angelica after you left. She helped me to understand some of your concerns."

Ivete lowered her brows.

He carried on without encouragement. "She explained how my actions made you feel. I want you to know how much I desire you." He reached for Ivete's hand and held it in his damp grasp. "I already told you, that woman means nothing to me. She was only temporary, a dalliance until you are ready for me." He sidled closer, and Ivete tried to wipe the grimace from her face.

Pain twisted in her belly as she remembered Della's words, how wrong she'd been to consider Thomas a dalliance of her own. She was more like Henry than she cared to admit, and his cool touch on her hand prevented her from forgetting him, though she wanted nothing more than that.

"I hoped, if you were feeling better, I might show you

how I care for you, how I desire you." He leaned in as though to kiss her.

Ivete placed a firm hand on his chest. "Desire me?"

"Yes. Angelica said Cynthie's revelation was most offensive and made you feel unwanted."

Ivete barked a laugh with no care for who heard. She'd love Henry to be caught in her room, professing his *desire*.

"I do not want you to show me your desire. I want nothing from you, save for you to release my hand and find your way back to your quarters and eventually your home."

"Ivete, you cannot—"

"I can do whatever I like. You are released from your commitment to me, and I hope you will release me as well. We are ill-fitted. As my mother has informed me, there are plenty of women who are willing to deal with your dalliances. I am not one of them."

She tugged her hand free from his grip and tried not to smile at his slack-jawed expression. The look of shock on his face did nothing to lessen his sharp features. Handsome and rich as the devil himself.

Yet Ivete felt no remorse at breaking their engagement. In fact, she felt only relief, release. "I wish you the best, Henry. Goodnight."

He slowly stood, his eyebrows knitting together.

When the door clicked closed again, she closed her eyes with a sigh. "Show me his desire," she muttered, shaking her head.

She slid to her pillow and under the blankets. Sleep, however, would not come. Her mind drifted from Henry to Thomas. The ability to tell him she was not engaged put a smile on her face, and she finally fell asleep at the prospect of what morning could bring.

20

_____

Ivete woke in the morning with a clear head and a smile on her face. Henry's attempt last night had been exactly what she needed to tell him how she felt. When she entered the kitchen, she was shocked to discover Bastien leaning against the countertop, whispering to his wife.

"Bastien?" Her heart lifted. On a morning such as this she might be glad to see anyone in that kitchen.

"I'm home. Sounds like you ladies missed me while I was away. And we've a full house."

"Yes." Ivete thought of Henry. _So full, some can't find their bed._

"I was telling Della I would ride out this morning and bring Eloise back with me. She said you've been doing a fine job in her absence."

"Your wife is kind but a poor liar."

Della laughed into the dough she was kneading. "You were better than no help."

"See? She tells the truth much better." Ivete helped herself to a scone from Bastien's plate. "When did you get here?"

"Last night. You missed the hustle."

"What do you mean?" Ivete popped the rest of the scone into her mouth and stepped around her brother to sink her hands into the warm, soapy water and scrub the tubful of dirty dishes.

"I mean Thomas and Willem birthed a foal then gathered the cows. They've already gone, headed to market."

"They?"

"Thomas and Otto Morris."

"Thomas is gone?"

"I tried to convince him to stay one day, get a full night's rest, but he couldn't be persuaded. He said we lost another cow while I was gone."

Ivete was silent, staring into the gray water. "Wait, did Willem go with him to market?"

"No. Father was the one who convinced Will not to go. I guess our pop has more experience massaging his children to his will."

Bastien stepped to Della and pressed his lips to the spot on her neck just below her ear. "If Willem asks, tell him I've gone for Eloise."

Ivete regretted taking her eyes from her work. Seeing their affection was the last thing she wished to witness. With Thomas so far away, her heart was heavy in her chest. Bastien and Della's devotion to one another made her feel hollow.

Once he was gone, Della joined Ivete with the dishes. "Are you okay?"

Ivete took a moment to think. "I guess so. What if he doesn't get back before I go?"

"What if he does?" Della didn't have to ask who she meant. They both knew Thomas was the only *he* Ivete cared about.

Ivete tried to imagine what it would be like if he came back, probably much like it was yesterday. Henry would be here, and what could she promise anyway? Was she to propose marriage?

"What do I do?"

Della leaned her shoulder into Ivete in a sign of solidarity. "You've got ten or so days. You'll think of something."

"You give me entirely too much credit." Ivete laughed. "*A fine help.* I can't believe you told Bastien that. He must have seen right through it."

"Not at all. Look at you, doing my dishes. You may not think it, but you have a knack for this. You see a task and aren't afraid to dive in and try it out. You're more capable than you know."

"I only wish I were more capable with words or decisions. I think my floundering might have lost me Thomas."

"No one is lost for good, Evie. That man has feelings for you. If he didn't, he wouldn't have been so upset. You just need to decide what your feelings are. Do you want him as a friend? Someone to ride with when you come to visit? Or is it more?"

"I want it to be more." Was *more* truly possible? Ivete's voice slid into an almost whine. "What am I going to do? Marry him and be a rancher's wife? I may be able to wash dishes, but I cannot cook like you can, nor scrub clothing without wrecking it."

"Is that the only obstacle? Cooking? Cleaning?"

The dishes were done, and both women dried their hands. Ivete lifted the heavy tub, and Della led the way, opening the front door so she could toss the water into the tall grass.

"Not the only one. My parents want me to marry Henry." The memory of last night dropped like a curtain into her mind. "After a prospect like Henry, they aren't going to accept my marriage to someone like Thomas."

Della put her hands on her hips and cocked her head at Ivete. "Now we're getting somewhere."

Ivete lowered her brows, waiting for more.

"You want to marry Thomas?"

Ivete laughed. "I can't just *choose* who I want to marry."

Della linked her arm with Ivete's. "This is the west. A woman can, in fact, choose her husband. Did you know a day's ride south, women have the vote? They've had it in Wyoming since 1869. Sit down. I want to tell you my story."

The two women sat at the table and ate their breakfast undisturbed while Della conveyed her unique courtship with Bastien. A time filled with Wanted posters and bounty hunters and snowed-in cabins.

When the story was done, Ivete possessed a new layer of respect for Della. The way she went after what she wanted and fought for herself.

"It's different, though. You were used to a certain life. Bastien was elevating your life. Can I really marry down?"

"No. I suppose you cannot." Della's tone was harsh. She stood and set her plate in the now-empty dish bucket. "I need to tend to Violet." She strode from the room.

Ivete heaved a sigh, angry with herself for speaking such harsh, thoughtless words, even if they were true. With one sentence, Ivete had unintentionally insulted both Della and Thomas, two of the people she cared about most. She didn't have to wallow for long before Willem joined her.

"Good morning." His smile was as wide as ever. "I helped birth a foal last night."

"I heard." She frowned and looked at the door he'd just entered through. It led to the bedrooms, not the guesthouse. "Did you sleep inside?"

"Yes. You chose a poor night to go to bed early. Bas returned with Della's friend and her children. They are in the guest house, and I'm bunking with your beloved. By the way, he snores." Willem chose an apple from a bowl on the counter and rubbed it against his vest.

"He's not my beloved." There were many things Ivete was unsure of, but Henry was not one of them.

"No? You should tell *him*." He took a bite of the apple with a loud crunch.

Ivete held back from telling Willem she already had. No use getting Henry beat up for his ill attempt at seduction.

"Where is everyone?" Willem glanced around the empty area.

"I wondered the same. Maybe the excitement from last night has worn everyone down."

"Not me." Willem beat his chest. "Actually, I hoped my sister would take me fishing, show me a thing or two."

"Sure," she replied. Della was apparently angry with her, and Eloise would be here to do the work. She had nothing else to do. "Let's go see if Bastien has a spare pole."

———

AT THE LAKE, Willem tied the horses while Ivete assembled the rod and line that they would be sharing.

"Did you bring a shovel for bait?" Willem called.

"I have flies on my hat." She'd adopted the office hat as her own and used the band to hold her flies.

Willem jogged to her side. "Digging for worms is part of the fun."

"Maybe, but baiting a worm hook isn't. Plus, we can use worms if we decide to fish along the creek later." The conversation transported Ivete back to her early fishing days at their grandparent's home. "I don't remember digging for worms at Grandfather's."

Willem chuckled. "You wouldn't. The servants did it for you."

Ivete sniffed. Worms were one of the many things that had been done for her without any understanding of the sacrifice. "Things are different out west. Here, we're both servant and guest."

"Sure are. I'm already beginning to wonder how often I can make the trip. There is something about it out here, and it's not just Della's cooking. I tell you, there's money in a gentleman's ranch."

Ivete cast her line and glanced at Willem. "Could you stay here indefinitely?"

Willem gave her a thoughtful frown. "I could. Don't know if I'd want to." He wagged his eyebrows at her. "You thinking about it?"

She turned back so he couldn't read her face. "I don't know." Willem was funny and wild, the youngest brother everyone worried about. Beneath his playful demeanor, though, he possessed a keen eye that missed nothing. He'd caught Ivete in a lie more than once because he could read her face as well as he could read a headline.

"This about Thomas?"

Ivete whirled around. She tried to decipher his face but couldn't. "What did he tell you?"

His blank face turned smug. "Nothing. You just did."

A fish tugged, and Ivete yanked the pole to set the hook before reeling the creature in.

Willem waded into the water to net the catch and gave Ivete a nod of approval. He sloshed back to Ivete. "Does Bas stock this lake?"

"He hasn't told me so. I'm just that good." She passed the

pole to him and turned to clean her fish. Once she was done, she gathered rocks to form a sort of pool and lay the fish in the water to keep cool while they continued fishing.

After several tries, Willem got a good cast and walked closer to Ivete. "So, what is it between you and Thomas?"

Ivete shook her head, angry that she'd given herself up so easily. "Can you read me so well?"

"Not just you. Thomas too. You two shared more than one loaded look, and I didn't dare ask *him*."

Ivete couldn't remember the looks he spoke of, but it wasn't a surprise that Willem picked up on some of it with all that was flying between them.

"So?" Willem urged.

"I don't know that anything is going on between us. Henry's appearance stopped anything that might have been."

"A fiancé does kill the mood."

Ivete smacked his arm. "You men brought reality to Aster Ridge. Whatever it was between Thomas and I, it was too fragile to withstand an ounce of pressure."

"Hmm. I like the man."

Ivete snorted. "Of course you do. He's like some Greek god to you. The god of birthing foals and herding cattle."

Willem's laugh soothed Ivete's heavy heart. "If there is a god of birthing foals, I ought to name my club after him."

Ivete laughed at her dreamer of a brother. "It would be a goddess. Don't forget the mare's small role in the birth of her colt."

Willem's face fell into thoughtfulness. "Nobody wants to join a club named after a woman. Not unless it's a madam."

Ivete stood and dried her hands on her skirt. "Does everyone, except me, know of these clubs in Chicago? It's like, one moment I'm an innocent who must be sheltered from all things, the next everyone is treating me like an ignorant fool."

"I never thought you a fool." He stepped closer and wrapped one arm around her. "I'm sorry. The joke was in poor taste."

She pushed him off. "You need to cast your line there." She pointed to the lake. "See how the water is darker in that section?"

It took him a few tries, but eventually, he landed his fly where he wanted it.

Ivete walked down the shore, away from Willem and his questioning. Was Thomas any better than Henry? Different maybe, but if he used club women how different could they be? She thought of his familiarity with that fancy woman on their trip to Aster Ridge. He may not take the time to leave the ranch and go into town for such services, but he'd used them during their travels. Did he always stop at the brothel while he was in town? Did it matter? Would he stop such behavior if they were together?

He may be friends with Bastien, but that didn't mean he viewed women and relationships the same as her brother did. Willem, her most wholesome brother had made a joke that told her maybe Willem was less wholesome than she thought. She tried to think of Thomas as a husband leaving for a brothel in town. A hotness burned in her belly and she knew she would do everything in her power to stop such a thing.

Something about the clean air and the rolling hills made her feel as though she had the power to stop him. A power she hadn't possessed in Chicago. It was just as Della had said: women had more out in the west. It was as though in Chicago she was a candle with a short wick and a servant waiting with a damper for the clock to strike. But here, she burned as brightly as she wished, and the forest provided plenty of firewood to keep her fed. It also gave her Thomas, and she wanted nothing more than to show him how brightly she could burn. Her flames danced only for him and she didn't care how much work it took to feed that flame.

21

—————

Thomas scrubbed the fatigue from his face and glanced at Otto. The boy's head hung forward and his limbs loose. He, too, was falling asleep in the saddle.

"We're almost there," Thomas reassured the boy. This was part of Thomas's worth to Bastien. He'd ridden all over the territory and knew the country well enough to move Bastien's cattle from vacant pen to vacant pen and lessen the likelihood of losing a curious animal on the way to market.

Once the herd was locked in, Thomas unbuckled his bedroll and laid it out. The sun was not yet down, but never had he been so drained. Between the birthing and rounding up the cows, his fatigued body weighed heavier with each mile they went.

He couldn't drive Ivete from his mind. It was as though he'd left a piece of himself there, with her, yet not enough to watch over her. She was making a mistake with Henry. The man wasn't worthy of her, yet Thomas was unable to find the words to tell her so. The further he got from Aster Ridge, the less angry he felt. Conviction replaced his anger. If she would only choose him, he wouldn't care about what she'd had with Henry in the past. He was already unsure how he would last until they'd sold the cows before turning his mount around and racing back to her.

22

_____

With so many guests, Ivete found it easy to avoid Henry. Lydia, Della's newly widowed friend, was warm, and her children brought a lightness that Ivete imagined Violet would lend soon enough. Her boy, Milo, was six and thought himself a man. He and Willem were partners, following Bastien around and lending help with Thomas's chores. Henry stuck close to her father, each of them being good sports when Willem wanted to see if other gentlemen thought one activity or another would be entertaining.

Ivete busied herself with chores she knew would appall Henry's city soul. Gathering eggs, for instance, required entering the often-odiferous chicken coop. Ivete had grown used to the smell, but Henry would likely rather travel on foot back to Chicago than have to endure it for any amount of time. Ivete plucked a final egg and exited the coop with a satisfied chuckle.

Her mother rushed toward her, arms clamped around Violet, her face fiercer than a thundercloud. "Henry has told your father the wedding is off."

Ivete sighed. With how much time they were spending

together, it was no wonder Henry had found the courage to tell Father. "This should not be a shock, Mother. Haven't I been telling you my intentions for several weeks now?"

"I thought you said you would wait until Chicago to make this decision. It isn't right to decide this when you're so far away from civilization."

"I disagree. I think here is the best place to think and consider what one wants out of life." She lifted her skirts to step over the threshold of the coop, latching the gate behind her with one hand while the other held the basket of eggs. "Even you have blossomed in Aster Ridge. I think you should plan a yearly stay. The fresh air does you good, as does a grandchild." Ivete stepped toward the house.

Her mother's arm shot out, holding her still. "Marrying for love is no promise of happiness."

Ivete shook the hay from the hem of her skirt. "No. I suppose one can never count on another for happiness." She placed a soft hand on her mother's arm and smiled at Violet. "It has warmed my heart to see the joy that baby brings you. I think perhaps we brought you the same joy, and I hope I might continue to do so."

Ivete walked to the house, the truth of her words sinking deeper until they touched her heart. She'd said the words to counter her mother's negativity, but they rang truer and louder the longer Ivete thought of them. Perhaps the only true way to happiness was to find it in herself first. If one relied too heavily for happiness on the approval of others, they'd be ... they'd be ... well, a bit like Ivete had been all her life—with no clue what she wanted or how to get it. An idea, shaped by words, grew in her mind. She did not need her parents' approval. She closed her eyes and inspected the idea. It felt good, like a weight lifted from her chest. Yes. She tried the words again, this time out loud, though whispered so only she could hear. "I do not need my parents' approval." The sweet freedom of the words made her want to cry.

She may have broken her chances with Thomas, but he wasn't the only thing to make her smile these many weeks. Working alongside Della, riding around the property, pulling fish out of the lake. All these things made her free in a way even visits to her grandparent's home did not. The happiness came from the idea that such a life was permanent and would not end when a carriage came to fetch her to Chicago. Now, just to convince Bastien to let her stay indefinitely.

AFTER DINNER, she and Della were tending the dishes with soapy hands when Bastien entered the kitchen. "Della says you wanted to speak with us."

Ivete gulped, reaching for a towel. "Yes."

Della stepped closer, forming a small circle. "We can finish these later. Let's speak in the entry."

The nights had grown chillier and being outside without a jacket was no longer comfortable. The entry was a wide corridor with two long pews on either side that once belonged to a churchhouse. Underneath one was Bastien's mud caked work boots accompanied by Willem's hardly used ones. The fact that Willem had purchased and brought a pair coaxed a smile from Ivete.

Bastien sat with his arm behind Della, without a care. Ivete wished she could go through life with confidence like Bastien possessed. Or better, she wished her life was such that she had reason not to stress. She cleared her throat.

"I wonder if I might stay a bit longer. Possibly indefinitely?"

Bastien didn't speak, but his eyebrows threatened to touch his hairline.

Della broke the tension. "I wondered if you might ask this. So, this is about more than traveling with Henry?"

Ivete sniffed. "He's done a fine job avoiding me this past week. It's nothing to do with Henry. It's more ... I love it here."

Bastien found his tongue. "That's because this is a holiday for you. We have to get back to our real lives. We cannot cater to guests indefinitely. And we have Lydia here now ..."

"I won't be a guest. I'll pull my load, and I'll help Lydia whenever she'll let me."

Della placed a hand on Bastien's knee. "Honey, Ivete is not a nuisance. Far from. I would dearly love the female company. I've grown used to it since Violet was born."

Both women looked at Bastien, their eyes wide and pleading.

He laughed. "I cannot say no to you." He planted a kiss on Della's lips. "If you want to fill our house with trouble, be my guest. Just don't be angry when things get tense and I head for the stables."

Della flashed a wicked smile at Ivete. "You've won. You'll have to sleep in Violet's room until Willem or Thomas leave."

"Willem?" Ivete asked.

Bastien answered, "Yes, it seems all my siblings are choosing to move the burden of chaperoning from our parents to me."

Della laid a hand atop Bastien's. "Willem has decided on

this Gentleman's Ranch endeavor and wants to stay a few more weeks to create a plan with Bastien."

Ivete's jaw dropped as she turned to her brother. "You're going into business with Willem?" The brother who rarely took life seriously. What benefit could Bastien possibly gain from such an endeavor with such a partner?

"I said I would help him figure things out. He wants to use my ranch for the business, at least to start. He can't very well invite gentlemen to build him a ranch."

"I wouldn't put it past him," Della teased.

Ivete stood to go.

"Oh, one thing," Bastien said, flicking his eyes to Ivete's vacated seat.

She sat back down.

"You have to tell Father. I'll not have him thinking I'm stealing all his children at once."

Ivete's throat went dry. She nodded, sinking further down the wooden bench. Bastien stood and extended a hand to his wife.

"This will be fun," Della said before allowing herself to be escorted away. Ivete stayed where she was, not eager to join the family and Henry by the fire.

———

THE NEXT MORNING Ivete sat next to her father at the breakfast table. "Would you like to take a ride with me this morning?"

He gave her a look of happy surprise. "I'd like that very much."

They finished their meal, and Ivete led the way to the stables. Once they were on their mounts and heading for the lake, her father spoke.

"Your mother tells me you are still set on denying Henry your hand."

"I am. Father"—she took a deep breath, trying to collect her words—"I cannot marry someone who isn't faithful. That is not the love I want. I understand marriage is forever, and I would be a fool to turn a relationship riddled with issues into a marriage."

He gave the same thoughtful frown that Bastien often made, and she was struck by how similar they were in appearance.

"I want different things now," Ivete said. "Not Henry and not Chicago."

"Chicago? Now, what could Chicago have done to earn your displeasure?"

His comment assured Ivete that her displeasure regarding Henry was no mystery.

"I love it here. I've asked, and Bastien and Della have given their permission for me to stay a bit longer."

Her father gave her a sidelong look. "You prefer the west to the city?"

Ivete nodded.

"I've worked all my life to give you children a beautiful life. Now three are abandoning me for a wild territory."

"Oh, Papa. You *have* given me a beautiful life. You've given all of us the opportunity to choose and a safe place to land when that choice was poor." If she weren't riding, she would hug him. Her heart was heavy with the idea of him thinking he'd done wrong by her.

"I'll agree, but I have one stipulation. Come home first."

"Papa, I—"

Her father lifted a hand, silencing her. "Your mother is convinced that you are caught up in a fantasy. A few months in real life would do you good."

"But how will I get back? Willem and Bastien are already here. Are *you* going to make the trip again so soon?"

"Heavens no, that is precisely why a man has sons. Luc can take you."

Ivete dipped her chin and gave him a withering glance. "Father, Luc is married now. You cannot command him at your whims."

He gave her a pointed look. "These whims are not mine. That is my final word on the matter. You may stay at Aster Ridge only if you return home first. You're likely in need of proper clothing anyways." He ran his gaze over the faded calico skirts she'd grown accustomed to wearing.

"And what if Luc refuses to accompany me?"

"You will make it back if I have to take you myself. You have my word."

Ivete sighed. "All right."

She'd gotten what she wanted, so why did she feel so defeated? And what would happen when Thomas returned from the market to find she'd left with Henry? Any hope she had of convincing him her intentions were true would be like ash in the wind. Could she risk that all for the whims of her father? But without her father's approval, he might rescind her dowry, and could she be happy living with even less than Della had?

23

As morning dawned on the day to leave for Chicago, Ivete dressed and ventured outside. Bastien loaded one of Ivete's trunks into the wagon while the other men stood in a circle speaking in low voices. Ivete watched how well Bastien played host. It was no wonder he was anxious for his guests to leave, to get his life back. Could Ivete really leave this life? She raised a flat hand to her forehead, searching the horizon for Thomas, her heart begging for his silhouette to come galloping across. How could she leave without seeing him? How could she leave at all? She needed the open sky and land more than she needed money. She might not be able to have Thomas if she couldn't bring money to the match, but it didn't matter. She couldn't leave here. Here was home. And if staying risked losing everything, she was willing to take that gamble. She was a Graham after all. Gambling was in her blood.

Ivete walked to the men and touched her father's arm. "Papa, I need to speak with you."

He smiled and wove her arm through his. "It is chilly out here. Let's talk inside."

Ivete allowed herself to be led into the entry where they could hear the clatter of Della preparing breakfast. Ivete faced her father and spoke softly in hopes their conversation would remain private. "I'll not be going home. At least not today."

Francis stepped away from her, glowering. "I thought we agreed."

"I did at first. But it doesn't feel right. And I'm old enough to make my own decisions."

He scrubbed at his chin. "Mother thinks you've taken a fancy to that livery man."

Ivete blinked at him, waiting.

"Your inheritance isn't such that you can marry anyone and be comfortable forever. Even Bastien's way of life isn't grand, and he's used his inheritance to set himself up."

The insinuation that she would still receive her inheritance if she went against him like this was a miracle. Her heart and her courage lifted.

He surveyed her with a hard eye, as though looking for a crack in her resolve. She took a deep breath and squared her shoulders.

Francis let out a long breath, and his shoulders drooped. "I see your mind is made up. I never wanted my daughter to be one of those sniveling girls, but I see I've done myself a disservice by preventing such. A little bit of deference would be nice." He pursed his lips as though suppressing a smile. "I should have at least kept you from reading those cheap cowboy novels." The grin stretching across his face softened his words.

Ivete flung her arms around his neck. "Thank you, Papa."

IN THE END, Ivete stood next to Della in the chilly yard as they said their heartfelt goodbye to her mother and father. Henry already sat astride his horse, and Ivete approached him. Her skirts were plain and her hair in a long braid over one shoulder. She looked up at him under the brim of the cowboy hat she'd taken to wearing whenever the sun was out. If Henry felt the loss of her while she looked thus, she would be quite surprised. She placed a hand on the horse's neck. "Thank you for making the trip. I hope you find happiness in Chicago."

He lifted his chin, not meeting her eyes. "I'm sure I will."

Ivete sighed and walked across the dusty gravel to speak with her father.

He placed a hand on her shoulder. "You're sure about staying?"

She smiled. "If I can't stand it, I'll send for you."

He chortled. "Unlikely. But a father can hope."

"You must bring Mother back at least once a year." They both turned and looked at her speaking with Della and admiring her granddaughter. She glanced up and caught Ivete's eye. With a sad smile, she came to stand next to Francis.

Ivete pulled her in for a hug, and her mother spoke into Ivete's shoulder. "Remember, you are Ivete Graham. No matter where you are, your worth is unchanging."

Those words were ones she had begun to wonder if she'd ever hear again. When the gossip about Ivete and the woman in the street began to spread, Ivete had been so ashamed. She'd thought herself an embarrassment to her family. Certainly she'd doubted her worth. Tears filled Ivete's lids. She swallowed a cry and pulled from her hug. "Thank you, Mama."

Once her father mounted his horse and was out of

earshot, her mother took Ivete's hands. "Willem will have rich men out here by the dozen. Don't settle for that cowboy just because he's handsome."

Ivete shook her head, but because she wasn't sure that cowboy would settle for *her*.

She returned to Della's side. They waved as the trio left to make the long trip home.

After a moment, Willem came over and draped an arm around Ivete's shoulders. "You're not on holiday anymore, Sis. How about you rustle up some breakfast for us hungry men?"

She jabbed him with her elbow. "You speak as though you are one of them, but your hands are not yet callused."

The group watched as the riders disappeared beyond the hills. Ivete expected to feel something, a pull to join them, but none came. She turned and followed Lydia and her children back into the house. Once inside, Lydia set her little girl down. Bridget was not yet a year and had mastered walking, though every step looked precarious.

"You're sure about this?" Lydia asked, jerking her head toward the retreating riders.

Ivete turned to her and drew a deep breath. "I'm sure, but it feels so final." She shook her head. Her feelings didn't even make sense to her. How would she explain? Though she could return home at any time, their leaving was like a death of sorts. The choice to go against her father's wishes affirmed her independence, and she would never count on them the same way again.

Lydia gave her a pat on the back, and they both moved into the kitchen. Eloise was there and had breakfast laid out. Milo, Lydia's boy, was already picking food from the serving plates, and Willem dished him food from the plates out of his reach.

"Milo," Lydia scolded. "Wait until we've said grace."

Ivete shot Willem a glance. He tucked his lips between his teeth and trained his gaze on the ceiling as though innocent.

Throughout their meal, Ivete's mind wandered like a lazy river. Bastien was right. She could not be a guest indefinitely. She wondered what her purpose could be on this ranch. How could she contribute in a way that was more than an assistant?

"When will Thomas be back?" Willem's voice cut into her thoughts. Her eyes flashed to Eloise, who had also perked up at the mention of Thomas.

Bastien leaned back into his seat, "In a few days, I suppose."

"I've yet to see you two working together. Are you as handy as him?"

Bastien laughed. "Not nearly. If I were, I wouldn't be giving him half my earnings."

"Half! By George, man. Whyever would you do that?"

"I needed his expertise. He was planning to start a venture of his own, and I had to make it worthwhile for him to stay."

"But fifty-percent shares?" Willem gave a long whistle.

"I don't need the money, but I do need a successful business to carry me through the years. Thomas can help me start that."

"So he won't be your partner forever, just until ..."

"When June comes, his contract ends."

It was November now. Ivete gulped. She had so little time left with Thomas. Della had suggested Ivete and Thomas might be only friends. Ivete did not like that scene one bit. The image didn't satisfy her, didn't ring true. But she would settle for friendship if it was all he would allow.

24

Thomas and Otto entered the Grahams' valley midmorning. The promise of a hot meal spurred them into a faster pace despite their fatigue.

Bastien walked out to greet them.

Thomas dismounted and walked with his friend. "Got a good price. Thirty-five a head."

Bastien stopped, his feet glued to the earth. "Thirty-five?" He lifted his hat and ran his hands through his hair. "How?"

Thomas continued walking, too tired to stop and talk. Bastien jogged to catch up. "We weren't the only ones losing cattle. Whatever it was, it swept through the state. There's less to buy. Therefore, what we brought in was worth more."

Bastien shook his head, wonder plain on his face. "I never thought we'd make up our losses."

Thomas shifted in the saddle, his body aching from the long ride. "We didn't quite."

"But close." A goofy smile spread on Bastien's face. "Della will be pleased."

"I'm sure Della has been fretting over cattle prices," Thomas teased.

"Thirty-five?"

Thomas laughed and broke away to lead his horse into the stable. He passed three empty stalls before he realized they were shut to the pasture. The horses were gone. A quick survey of the stable told him they were the beasts Francis, Willem, and Henry had brought. His heart dropped. He was too late. Ivete had gone home. He hardly lifted his eyes as he unsaddled and brushed down his mount. He looked up only to address Otto. "You'll feed them?"

Otto nodded.

Thomas walked toward the guest house, a hot meal no longer forefront in his mind. With how heavy his heart felt, only sleep would do.

"Ho!" Willem strode around the corner. "Bas didn't tell you? The fair Lydia resides in the guest house."

"Am I in the barn, then?" Thomas quipped, hoping Willem would point him in the right direction before exhaustion caused him to fall on his face.

"You're being paid too well to live in the barn. Della has you set up in the house. C'mon."

Thomas followed Willem along the length of the house until they reached the front door. "You're in Ivete's room. She's moved to the nursery."

"Ivete?"

Willem waved away Thomas's question. "She's fine. Violet still sleeps near Della anyways."

Willem left, a bounce in his step and Thomas waited for his sluggish mind to comprehend. He was certain those horses had left, their stalls not only empty but clean. The saddles had been gone, too.

Thomas swept through the front door.

Eloise was sweeping the entryway and startled. "Mr. McMullin. You're back." She glanced around herself. "You must be hungry." She spun, and he followed her to the kitchen. He fell into one of the dining chairs as she pulled a loaf of bread from the oven.

With quick fingers she plucked it from the tin and placed it on a plate in front of him. "My papa would always eat a full loaf after a trip. Said it didn't feel like home until my mother's bread was in his belly." She set a small jar of preserves in front of him as well as a knife.

"Thank you." He pulled the rustic meal closer and devoured the entire loaf, hot from the oven and fluffy as a cloud.

"Have the Grahams gone then?" he asked, plucking each crumb off the plate with the end of his finger.

"Yes. Left not three days ago."

"Ivete stayed behind?"

"She did."

Lost in thought, Thomas almost didn't notice Eloise appear at his side. "I'll take that." She slid the plate from between his elbows.

"Where is she now?"

"Ivete? I haven't seen her all morning."

He'd been entirely focused on the three missing horses. He didn't think to check if any others were gone from the stable. The idea of climbing back on a horse was torturous. He'd find her on foot.

"Thank you for the meal, Eloise. Your father is right. It was just what I needed."

He stood and made his way through the front door and to the stables. When he saw Dusty was out of her stall, he glanced at the wide opening to the stable, as though she would be there waiting for him. Dusty was Della's mare, and Bastien would not have let her be taken to Chicago.

Where should he begin his search? Didn't matter as long as he began. The desire to find Ivete felt like an itch that would never be satisfied until he laid eyes on her. What had kept her from returning to Chicago? An image came of her casting her line, and wearing his ruined hat, the band peppered with holes from her flies. Thomas began the long walk to the lake, quickening his step with each stride. The body of water was around a bend and out of sight from the house. Once around that rise, he saw her horse in the distance. He picked up his pace to a light jog as he approached. The cool weather meant the sun wasn't able to burn up the morning dew from the grass. As it swished against his legs it drenched his breeches up to his knees. He didn't care. His thoughts swirled with Ivete and the invisible lasso that tugged him closer to her.

He must have made a sound because she turned, her eyes wide. "Thomas?" She reeled in her pole and set it on the ground.

He kept his pace until she was within reach. He had to check himself from going further, rocking back on his heels and banding his arms to his sides. They wanted nothing more than to be around her, to hold her close.

Her cheeks held that rosy glow brought from a cold wind. "You're back."

He nodded. "You're still here."

"I am." She leaned closer but didn't step nearer. He watched her throat bob up and down.

"Why?"

She shook her head. "I couldn't go back. I didn't want to."

"Ever?"

"Not to live."

So, the wedding was off, then. And she was here. Against all odds, she *chose* to live here.

"What will you do now?" he asked.

"Catch fish to earn my keep."

He smiled, wishing he could reach out for her, wishing she would come to him. She glanced behind him. Her eyes traveled down to his wet ankles. "Did you walk here?"

"I've been in the saddle for nearly two weeks."

"What was so urgent it couldn't wait?"

Thomas opened his mouth but fear stopped his words.

Ivete stepped closer.

"You stayed." His words mingled with his exhale. He still struggled to believe her presence.

"I did."

"Why?"

She lifted a shoulder and gave a thoughtful frown. "A few reasons, but I was hoping you would give me one more." She lifted her eyes to meet his.

At her words, he yanked her into his arms, crushing his lips to hers. She wrapped her arms around him, pulling him closer and knocking his hat off in an attempt to knot her fingers with the back of his hair.

They laughed as the hat hit the ground. The kiss was over, but they remained in one another's arms.

He took her face in his hands. "You could be happy here?"

"I *am* happy here."

Reality hit Thomas. "But for good? Would you be happy staying here forever?"

"Do I have a reason to stay forever?" She twirled a lock of his hair at the base of his neck.

He caught her hand and loosened his grip around her

waist. "I cannot give you the things you are accustomed to having."

"You can give me something else entirely. It was Henry who could not give me what I wanted."

"You made that clear to him?" The last thing Thomas wanted was to be mixed up in another muddled commitment.

She nodded. " I did."

He pulled her in and pressed his lips to hers, softer this time as he explored her mouth and the way she surrendered to him. He thought of that night in the hallway, how she'd tried to give herself to him then. That night he'd used every ounce of willpower not to imagine all the things he wanted to do with Ivete. Now he had to use that willpower to resist the urge to lay her down on this isolated beach and do to her everything he'd tried not to imagine. Her horse snickered as though chiding their behavior. Ivete laughed and pulled out of the embrace. Thomas didn't know whether to thank the beast or curse it. Ivete's laughter rang like church bells around them. "No matter, Dusty," Thomas said, never taking his eyes from Ivete. "She's mine now, and that's all that matters."

25

Ivete woke early and joined Della in the kitchen. Eloise had returned, but Ivete still desired to be both helpful and capable.

Della had taught her to start a batch of bread the night before, and this morning, they would continue the process. When Della entered the kitchen, she looked like the undead. Her face was slack and her eyes red.

"Sprinkle some flour on the counter and pull the dough from the bowl," Della instructed with a yawn.

"Rough night?" Ivete asked.

Della gave a slow nod. "Turn it over several times, then return it to the bowl."

More kneading; it was no wonder Della had strong arms.

Another gaping yawn overtook her. "That's all for now. Now we get started on breakfast."

"Why don't you get back to bed? I can handle breakfast."

Della lifted one brow and looked at Ivete.

Ivete laughed. "I can."

"Let me at least get the stove started for you."

Once Della was gone, Ivete's confidence sank to the soles

of her feet. She couldn't remember ever being alone in this kitchen. It was the hub of Della's home, and someone was always inside, usually Della herself.

But Ivete had chosen to stay in the west, so she had to learn to do all Della could do and on her own, too. She rolled her sleeves up, gathered her confidence around her, and set to work. Gravy first. She scooped grease from a glass jar and scraped it into the cast iron skillet. Next, flour, which sat on the counter next to the bowl of dough. Once the gravy was bubbling, she turned to make biscuits.

Eloise, too, had joined in on Della's biscuit lesson. Biscuits weren't something Chef ever made back home, but Ivete doubted even he could compare. Ivete's completed dough was stickier than Della's. She bit her fingernail. Adding more flour would help, right? But if she added too much, that could ruin all her hard work. No more flour, then. She rolled the dough flat, cut them out the best she could, and checked the thermometer inside the oven. She added another log, then the pan of biscuits. She bustled across the kitchen to the gravy. Hm. Lumpy. She whisked then whisked even harder. No luck. The chunks remained no matter what she did.

She frowned at the pan, wondering if she could salvage it or if she should start again.

Before she could decide, the front door opened, and Ivete heard Willem's voice. He came around the corner, Thomas at his side. They both stopped short, gaping at her.

"Good morning." Thomas smiled, stepping nearer. "We hoped breakfast was ready." His eyes wandered from the kitchen to the empty living area.

"I'm making breakfast. Della is resting from a difficult night with Violet."

Willem scoffed. "Oh, boy. I think we'd have been better

off eating oats from the stable. C'mon, let's see if Lydia will feed us." He turned back the way he came.

Ivete's heart sank, and her eyes followed suit. It was just as well since her lumpy gravy would only prove Willem right. The front door clicked again, but when she picked herself back up, Thomas was still there.

"Can I help?"

Ivete gave a hard laugh. "Can you salvage bad gravy?"

He smiled and stepped up to the stovetop. He stirred the gravy and lifted the pan from the heat. "This isn't too far gone. Do you have any more milk?"

Ivete brought it to him.

He poured in a small amount and whisked. His quick movements pulverized the lumps, and it was smooth once again. "Leave it off the heat, or it will get lumpy again."

Ivete shook her head. She wanted to wrap her arms around him, but she had biscuits in the oven and a point to make. Instead, she moved around and peeked at the biscuits. Almost done.

"I may not be able to make it, but I can serve it. Sit down." Ivete gestured to the table, and he obeyed.

She placed cut apples and persimmons on a plate and grated cinnamon over the top before setting it in front of him. Her biscuits had turned golden, and she put two on a plate and covered them in gravy. She stood with her hands on her hips, watching him, waiting to see if he liked it.

When he nodded his approval, she released a sigh of relief. She made herself a plate and joined him at the table.

"It's like a ghost town without my mother and father here. I never realized how our visit doubled the number of people on the ranch." She took a bite. The food wasn't nearly as good as Della's, but it was edible.

"Bastien is sleeping, too. He came out to milk, then told me Willem would have to be my help today."

"I didn't even hear Violet. Did you?"

Thomas shook his head.

Willem returned, Milo at his heels. Lydia and Emmeline brought up the rear.

"I heard you needed help with breakfast." Lydia's eyes took in the breakfast spread across the counter. "But from the looks of it, I've come too late. You've already done all the work."

Ivete returned to the kitchen and helped dish plates for the children. When Willem grabbed a plate, Ivete pulled the pan of biscuits out of reach. "I think you mentioned wanting oats for breakfast."

Willem smirked and with deft movements caught her by the waist and grabbed a biscuit off the pan. Ivete laughed as her chest swelled with pride. She had fed these people, and the breakfast she'd made was decent.

As they finished their meal, Eloise arrived. She took a look at the bread in the bowl and lifted the towel off to continue the breadmaking process. Ivete watched her, so at ease in the kitchen. She didn't need to ask anything, just one look at the bread, and she knew if it was ready for the next step. A frown tugged at the corners of Ivete's mouth.

Lydia hitched her voice. "Good morning, Eloise dear. That is Ivete's loaf. She's going to finish it up today."

Eloise nodded and gave Ivete a small smile before returning the towel to its place and getting started on the dishes.

"Thank you," Ivete mouthed to Lydia.

Lydia winked.

Ivete scowled at her brother. "Does Willem often barge into your home demanding breakfast?"

Lydia laughed. "Not often, but now he's thought of it, I wonder if I'll ever be rid of him."

Willem dropped his fist on the table at their mockery. "Can't a guy get a decent meal these days without any grief attached?"

They laughed, and Della entered the room, Violet in her arms. She looked less tired, though she'd only had an hour more of rest. How much of that time had been spent nursing the babe?

Ivete stood and held out her arms. "Let me take her."

Della nestled Violet into Ivete's arms and then heaved a tired sigh. Bastien came behind Della and kissed the top of his wife's head.

Eloise brought two plates from the kitchen and set them at the empty seats. Everyone sat down again. Every seat at Della's table was filled.

Ivete cuddled her niece. The child's sleeping face was like that of an angel's. "You'll need another chair once Violet grows into one."

Della laughed. "Bastien is already pining for another."

Bastien laughed through his mouthful of food. Swallowing quickly, he said, "Not now. Just another in general." He ran a knuckle down his wife's cheek, and any bitterness Della may have feigned disappeared.

When they showed their love like that, Ivete had to move her gaze away, afraid to intrude on a private moment. Her eyes fell on Lydia, whose lips pressed together in a tight line. Bridget squawked, and Lydia blinked out of her haze and smiled as she fed her little one.

What must Lydia's life have been like to cause her such grief? Her husband must have been good enough to be held in high esteem by Bastien. Would she ever be able to find another man to compare? Milo's belly laugh drew Ivete's gaze. He and Willem had their heads together, no doubt planning their adventures for the day. Willem seemed to have an affinity for the young boy, but he'd never shown interest in children before. Maybe he liked Milo because he could relive his own youth through adventures with the boy.

After breakfast was cleared, the men left the house. When Ivete's bread making lesson was over, Della shooed her outside for a ride.

"You need the exercise. Your energy is making me tired."

"Your daughter is the one stealing your energy, not me." Ivete laughed as she turned to the stables.

She found Thomas in the office, with Willem. "Thomas, care for a ride? What good is this one"--she pointed a thumb at Willem—"if he doesn't allow you to get away once and a while?"

Thomas smiled at her, and his eyes crinkled. He tipped his hat at Willem and came to Ivete. She led the way around the corner. When they were out of Willem's sight, she stopped to pull him in for a kiss.

Willem walked out of the office and gave a disgusted groan.

Ivete and Thomas broke apart and laughed.

As he retreated, he called over his shoulder. "If you're going to do that, you're going to have to marry her."

"I intend to," Thomas whispered against her lips.

EPILOGUE

I vete tried her best to assimilate into the daily work of the ranch. She was given sole care of the chickens' welfare, which meant she'd taken a dislike to foxes and wished for Bastien to allow her to use his .22 rifle. He doubted her ability with the weapon and told her to stick to fishing.

She raised her eyes to the horizon, searching for a lone rider with Thomas's frame. She laughed at the reality of her being left in Montana while Thomas made the trip to Chicago. He'd insisted on asking her father for her hand, convinced that doing so in-person was the right choice. Meanwhile, more than a week had passed. Ivete waited anxiously for his return.

In the short time since Lydia had arrived, Ivete had grown to love the widow's companionship. While Della's strengths were in cooking, Lydia excelled at sewing and mending. She helped Ivete make a wardrobe of her own, since Della was beginning to fit into her old clothes again.

Ivete kept her eyes on the ridge line as the day wore on. Thomas's letter had said he'd return on Tuesday, and she didn't expect him in the morning, but as the day wore on, she couldn't stop herself from searching for him. Thomas's letter had been irritatingly vague. He gave no clue as to what her father said. Had he accepted Thomas's plea for Ivete's hand? Had he turned Thomas out on his ear? Had Mother thrown a fit about Ivete marrying someone without wealth or status? She worried her lip all day until it grew sore to the touch.

She and Lydia were in the guest house. Ivete was putting in the final hem on her new dress, while Lydia coached her to keep the thread tight, or to smooth the fabric tighter. Lydia was a fine seamstress and had brought material with her. When she'd learned Ivete was living in borrowed gowns, she'd insisted on making a dress for Ivete. Ivete had equally insisted that Lydia teach her how to make the dress.

Ivete wanted to laugh at how much time she and Lydia had spent as they finished this project. No doubt much more than Lydia had anticipated when she agreed to help teach Ivete to sew. She looked up from her work to smile at Lydia. "I appreciate your patience, but this was much more difficult than I imagined. I'm doubtful I could ever replicate it without your assistance."

"Della knows a bit, and you can always buy one in town. With all the Grahams are doing for me and my children, I wanted to give back, and this is my specialty. I can help you with curtains once you and Thomas get set up with a house of your own. Curtains are easy."

Ivete snipped the end of her thread and shook out the dress. The material was a cotton gingham with blue and white checks, absolutely country. Ivete loved it. "When my grandfather taught me to fish, he did so that I might have my own source of entertainment on our visits to their home. My brothers were always galavanting together, and I had no sister for a companion. I had never expected it to turn into such a practical skill. I imagine sewing is a more practical skill, and I'm determined to learn it. Will you fetch me any time you are working on something? Even watching will do me good."

Lydia chuckled. "I'd be happy to."

At that moment, Willem and Milo came galloping past the large window that looked into the yard.

Ivete shook her head. "Milo won't need a brother so long as Willem is near."

Lydia's face softened. "Milo could use a bit of lightness. Unfortunately, we won't be able to stay for long." She sighed and stood, tidying the bric-a-brac of their project. "Go try on the dress. I want to see it on. You can show Thomas when he returns."

Ivete scampered to the back bedroom, the very space where Rodgers had taken her hostage. She checked every corner of the space before calming her heart and removing her borrowed clothes. How was it Lydia stayed here alone? She should be in the big house. What if Rodgers returned. Or Harder. Or some unknown danger. She shook her head. Was she mad for loving it out here? As Ivete worked the small buttons that ran up the front she admired herself in Lydia's mirror. The blue of the dress made her pale gray eyes brighter, much like this valley brightened her spirits. She may not be the most beautiful, or the kindest, or the bravest, but while she was here, she felt she was all those things. Thomas's appreciative looks made her feel beautiful, and her own constant need to help her family made her feel kind. She didn't mind being in the service of others, didn't mind mustering her courage to walk to the henhouse in the dark or pluck a dead chicken from the ground when a pesky fox had found its way inside.

Possibly for the first time in her life, she genuinely liked who she was. Instead of walking into a room and eyeing the inhabitants to make sure she was the better of the group, she no longer had a desire to compare. She had found worth inside of her, and what others thought didn't matter.

She returned to the living area with a twirl, showing off her new dress to Lydia. Wonderful Lydia, whom Ivete might have once thought herself above. Ivete shook her head, a small gesture of disbelief. The woman was going through unimaginable pain. She was kind and generous, yet the only time she smiled was when Willem had pulled out every one of his charms. He acted as though it were his personal mission to make her laugh.

Lydia nodded. "It looks lovely. The color is much more suited to you than to me."

Ivete smiled. "I do love the color. I'll send you some fabric from Chicago. My seamstress is the best at matching coloring. I'll tell her yours, and we'll send you something perfect."

Lydia shook her head. "Please, don't. This was old fabric; I would have given it away had Bastien not had ample space in his wagon."

Ivete imagined losing her husband, and immediately vacating the home where they'd lived. "Could you not have stayed on in Kirwin?"

Lydia shook her head. "No single women are allowed in the town, and besides they needed the cabin for Simon's replacement." She looked out the window as though turning over a memory. A smile stretched on her face and Ivete hoped the woman had plenty of happy memories to sustain her through the hardship of widowhood.

Lydia said, "I think your brother wants us."

Ivete's attention wandered from her new friend to the

figure of Willem jogging toward them. He carried Milo on his shoulders, and both waved their arms in the air. She peeked at Lydia once more. Had that smile been for Willem and not some happy memory?

Rather than use the door, Willem and Milo came right to the window and called through the glass. "Thomas is coming!"

Ivete's breath hitched. She rushed out the door. He was far off, but clearly riding hard for the ranch. She laughed, thinking of when he'd returned from escorting Eloise home on the night of Aaron's arrival. She imagined he might have looked something like this as he rushed back to them. To her.

Della and Eloise stepped out from the main house. Ivete glanced around to find no horses were saddled. Instead she walked toward him, planning to meet him far enough away that they might have a reunion with only eyes on them and not ears as well.

She lifted her skirts, newly aware of the effort it took to make a hem and not inclined to damage her hard work.

When Thomas reached her, he slid off the saddle and took her hands. He put one knee on the ground. His eyes shining, his cheeks bright from the cold wind on his face as he looked up at her. "Ivete Graham, will you be my wife?"

Her breath caught in her throat. She tugged her hands from his and sat on his knee, throwing her arms around his neck. She pulled away and looked into his eyes. "He said yes?"

"I was a bit more concerned about *you* saying yes."

Ivete tossed her head. "Yes. Of course, yes!"

Thomas pressed his lips to hers, but Ivete knew he wanted to marry her. What she didn't know was if her father was going to bless the marriage, or give them her dowry.

Ivete spoke into Thomas's lips. "What did he *say*?"

Thomas laughed. "He said yes."

Ivete took a shuddering breath. She hadn't realized how afraid she'd been. Not until that moment. "Of course he did. You're a fine match for any girl."

Thomas smiled and it warmed her heart. "Not quite. He had much to say about my ability to support you."

Ivete's gaze flashed to Thomas's. "Will he give us my dowry?"

"He had stipulations."

Ivete scoffed. Always a negotiation with papa. She should have gone with, no doubt she knew better how to bend her father to her will. "What are his demands?"

"A six month engagement and you go to Chicago for ninety days to plan the wedding, which will take place there."

"Ninety days?" Ivete groaned. "He makes me sound like a late fee. Surely—" But she stopped her objections. It might very well take three months to have a dress made by Madame McPike's due to her waitlist. She shook away the thought and twisted her mouth. "I don't care about a Chicago wedding."

Thomas took her face in his hand, "Shall we marry without his blessing?"

"Of course not. Just when I get out from under his thumb, he pins you down." Ivete looked heavenward. Her father was a hard man. And if Thomas had already agreed to his requirements, Ivete would have to go along with them, or make the trip to Chicago just to argue. She tried no to sound deflated as she said, "That means you can start on your ranch right away. Bastien will release you from your commitment to him."

Thomas cocked his head, a whisper of a smile on his lips. "I'm not so sure I need to be released."

Ivete's eyebrows drew together as she waited for more information.

"Bastien has offered to sell us land along the south end. We'll be close enough to continue working with one another."

A weight Ivete hadn't realized she'd been holding slid away. She'd be close enough to ask Della's assistance in whatever chore she had to learn. "Will that be enough land for you?"

Thomas lifted the wide of his mouth in that self-assured way. "The Morrises are willing to sell a portion when we are ready."

When Thomas had her dowry in hand. "That's wonderful." And it was. The tears that pricked Ivete's eyes proved her happiness. She threw her arms around his neck and held him close, breathing in his peppermint smell mixed with the metallic tang of the outdoors.

She drew away. "You must be famished."

He kept one arm around her and the other led the horse as they walked to the house. "Is this a new dress?"

Ivete grinned. "You are observant, Mr. McMullin."

"Yes, well, I've learned to keep my eye on you." He gave her a squeeze and released her to greet the group that was waiting to welcome him home.

ABOUT THE AUTHOR

Kate Condie is a speed talker from Oregon. Reading has been part of her life since childhood, where she devoured everything from mysteries, to classics, to nonfiction—and of course, romance. At first, her writing was purely in journal format as she thought writing novels was for the lucky ones. She lives in Utah and spends her days surrounded by mountains with her favorite hunk, their four children and her laptop. In her free time she reads, tries to learn a host of new instruments, binge watches anything by BBC and tries to keep up with Lafayette as she sings the Hamilton soundtrack.

ALSO BY KATE CONDIE

Also by Kate Condie

Aster Ridge Ranch

Ticket to Anywhere

A Winter's Vow

A Cowboy's Vow

A Widow's Vow

A Bandit's Vow

Want free content and more from Kate Condie? Sign up for her newsletter or follow her on social media @condie.kate